Journey to the Underground World

LIN CARTER

Illustrated by *Josh Kirby*

DAW BOOKS, INC.

DONALD A. WOLLHEIM, PUBLISHER
1633 Broadway
New York, N.Y. 10019

FIRST PRINTING, NOVEMBER 1979

1 2 3 4 5 6 7 8 9

DAW TRADEMARK REGISTERED
U.S. PAT. OFF. MARCA
REGISTRADA. HECHO EN U.S.A.

PRINTED IN U.S.A.

Since I am not at liber which this first volume of .... came into my hands, I can hardly expect my readers to consider it as anything more than a work of fantastic fiction.

I have known Carstairs off and on for several years. Although the rugged young adventurer is many years my junior, we seem to have hit it off from the start. Perhaps that is because he lives the sort of action story I usually write: I envy him the zest for living and appetite for experience which marks his exciting career, and he seems to admire my abilities as a writer.

In preparing this first book of his manuscript for the press, I have divided the narrative into chapters to which I affixed titles of my own devising. Other than those minor tasks, the book as it now stands is very substantially the same as that which was given into my hands by a member of his family. Perhaps at some later occasion I may be permitted to discuss how the memoir came into my possession. That decision remains to be made by Carstairs' family, who control literary rights to his papers.

Frankly—and I admit this wistfully—I would like to believe that what is written here is true, although I cannot vouch for the veracity of the tale. A hopeless romantic such as your editor would enjoy knowing that, in this increasingly mundane world of ours, there are still lost lands in the remote corners of the earth where fantastic monsters roam, where noble and chivalrous men battle against terrific odds, where chaste and beautiful women remain to be rescued from sneering villains, and where adventure and peril and heroism thrive amid exotic and bizarre scenery.

If you thrive on such fare—truly the "stuff that dreams are made of"—then follow Eric Carstairs into Zanthodon, the Underground World, and share in the fantastic marvels and perils and splendors whose truth only he can know.

—LIN CARTER

"We are witnessing a combat no human eyes ever looked on before!"

Part One

THE LOST LAND

Chapter 1.

EAST OF SUEZ

It was the glint of steel in the folds of the red burnoose that caught my eye—the bright flash of sunlight on a naked dagger!

It was just half an hour before noon, in the native quarter of Port Said. I can be precise about the time because I recall that even as I glimpsed the glitter of bare steel, the ululating cry of the *selâm* was echoing from where the *mueddin* stood on the gallery of the little mosque behind me. And it was a Friday, for that wailing cry, that humble salute to Allah, is chanted forth upon that day and in that hour all across the East, and thus it has been for generations beyond the numbering. . . .

The midday sun was roasting and the air was dry as dust and reeked of amazing stenches: goat urine and unwashed men and cooking sausages and raw onions and heady musk and sweet sandalwood and the fresh dung of camels. A medley of odors that, to me, will always say—*Egypt*.

In the square before me surged a gaudy throng. Brown children shrieked and chased each other; mongrels growled over scraps of garbage, a lemonade merchant jangled his tin cups not unmusically; women robed and veiled in black, with only their *kohl*-rimmed eyes visible, shrilled as they fought down the price of bright cloth with a fat, fez-hatted shopkeeper; French girls in light frocks from the cruise ship moored in the harbor poked through a wooden tray of silver bracelets and turquoise brooches; oblivious to the noise, the stenches, the milling crowd, an elderly gentleman sat cross-legged under a striped awning, sipping tea with the serene dignity of a graven Ramses; two swarthy Armenians haggled over an opal large as a human eye.

I had caught that bright flash of naked steel from the corner of my eye. Turning in the same instant, I peered into the

11

mouth of a narrow alleyway behind the mosque. It was black as the Styx and choked with putrid garbage. But not so black that I could not see the three men who struggled there: and even the reek of rotting garbage could not drown the cold and bitter smell of villainy and red murder—

I sprang upon the taller of the red-robed men and knocked him face down on the slimy cobbles—turned to seize the bony dark wrist of the second man with my left hand, twisting it until the hooked dagger dropped to clang upon the paving stones while I drove the balled fist of my right into his lean belly.

He paled to the hue of sour milk, sank to his knees, eyes rolling up to display bloodshot whites, then folded forward and began noisily to lose his breakfast. Stepping to one side I put my booted foot on the dirty wrist of the first assassin, who was worming stealthily toward the fallen knife; his wrist bones crunched under my weight and he squealed like a gutted lamb. Then I reached for the third man they had been about to mug, caught him by an upper arm and rapidly propelled him out of the fetid darkness and into the clamor and bustle of the marketplace.

He blinked at the dazzling impact of the noontime sun and tottered woozily, panting to recover his breath. I looked him over. He was an odd, comical little man, very thin and quite a bit shorter than I, and somewhere in his sixties as far as I could judge. He was dressed in stained, disreputable khaki shorts and a safari shirt, both several sizes too big for his scrawny frame. A huge, old-fashioned sun helmet covered most of his bony, baldish head. His pointed nose supported a pair of antiquated nose-glasses—*pince-nez*, I think they are called—these teetered insecurely and were often askew.

His eyes were large and watery and blue, under tufted, snowy brows, and looked curiously out of place in his leathery tanned face, which was bony and long-jawed. A stiff little tuft of white goatee jutted from the point of his chin, and a white mustache bristled from his upper lip, creating the illusion of a Vandyke. When he spoke, his voice was high-pitched, querulous, with an Oxford accent; and he spoke in a rather verbose, slightly pompous, very pedantic manner.

"Holy Heisenberg!" he wheezed. "You arrived in the very nick of time, young man!"

"Are you okay?" I inquired. "Did they get your wallet?"

"Eh? Wallet . . . ?"

I nudged his bony hip, felt a reassuring flattish bulge. How the two thieves had lured the old fellow into that dark alley I did not bother to inquire: he looked so absent-minded and unworldly and easily bamboozled, there was no reason to inquire. So I took his arm again, propelled him a quarter way around the square and into the cool dimness of the Cafe Umbala. The Nubian waiter, who knew me well, grinned, white teeth flashing in his ebony face, amused, doubtless, at the odd couple we made. The little man in soiled khaki kit came only to my armpit; he was thinner than the legendary rail, and my weight could have made three of him, or nearly. He waggled a stiff white goatee in my direction and attempted a jerky little bow, which made his old-fashioned sun helmet fall over his bald brow, knocking his glasses askew.

"Your unexpected assistance, sir, was timely and most welcome," he said breathlessly. "Those two ruffians—!"

I drew him to a seat behind a tiny table set against a wall of flaking plaster adorned with posters advertising such varied amusements as a Parisian *chanteuse*, who really hailed from Constantinople, a Chinese magician who was actually an ex-Brooklyn cardsharp of pure Gypsy descent, and a brand of liquor fermented from overripe prunes and fit, from my experience, only for removing old paint from cheap furniture.

"Relax—catch your breath, pop," I counseled. At my elbow the Nubian waiter materialized like a genie from the *Arabian Nights*: "Dry mahtini, *sah*?"

"Yep, Tabiz, the usual," I said. "What's your poison, old timer?"

The white tuft of goat-beard jutted skyward stiffly and I received a frosty glare. "Potter is the name, my good man—Professor Potter."

"Okay, Doc, have it your way," I grinned. "But what'll you have?"

He sniffed sharply. "As a rule, I do not indulge . . . still and all, I suppose . . . under the circumstances . . . just to restore the tissues . . . for medicinal purposes only, you understand! . . . under the advice of my physician . . . a drop or two of spiritous beverage can do no harm, surely?"

"Surely," I nodded.

"Straight gin," he snapped at the waiter. "Gordon's, if you stock it; Boodle's will do."

It turned out to be Old Mr. Boston, but gin (I have found) is gin.

We talked over our drinks. For the past two months I had been out "east of Suez" as Sax Rohmer or Talbot Mundy would put it, in the desert country in Sinai, performing some rather delicate shipping flights in an old Sikorsky chopper supplied me by a Greek importer.

Let's not mince words: I'd been smuggling out antiquities for a fellow named Pappadappoulas who daren't risk trying to get the stuff out through customs. Nothing much, just broken pottery and a couple of chewed-up Syro-Roman busts; anyway, the Greek either defaulted or got busted and I found myself with about seventy dollars American in my jeans and the proud owner of a beatup Sikorsky, which was probably also hot. As I carelessly filled the Professor in on my recent business venture, he interrupted me with excitement written all over his whiskery visage:

"A *helicopter*, you say, my boy? Great Galileo!—how utterly fortuitous! Does it . . . ah . . . is the vehicle in skyworthy condition?" he inquired breathlessly, a feverish glint in his watery optics.

I shrugged. "A drop of oil here and there and the other place, and a full tank of the best octane, that's all it needs. We needed the chopper, you understand, 'cause we had to fly low. Mr. Sadat's customs men use radar now, and the border country fringes some on Israeli-held territory. Antiaircraft batteries, you know . . . and trigger fingers get mighty itchy in that part of the world . . ."

Something like prophetic bliss shone in his misty eyes. An adam's apple the size of a golfball wobbled up and down in his stringy throat, measuring the intensity of his emotion just as the mercury does in a thermometer.

"When you saved me from those scalawags, my boy," he said huskily, I thought . . ." And he rattled off a line or two of Swahili. Well, it was pure Swahili as far as *I* was concerned; it turned out to be Greek.

Then he cleared his throat apologetically: "Hem! Forgive me, lad . . . Simonides the Athenian . . . 'One welcomes the

CONTENTS

List of Illustrations

arrival of a friend in need, even if he be a stranger at the time.' "

"You don't have to—"

He silenced me with a magnificent gesture. "Not at all! The poet echoed my feelings of the moment; but now that I learn you possess a helicopter, I feel, rather (with Ephialtes), 'Be serene: the Gods will provide you with the thing you need, in the hour appointed—' "

He leaned forward suddenly, as if to transfix me with that white spike of stiff beard.

"Have you ever heard of Zanthodon?" he whispered hoarsely.

Of course, I hadn't; nor has hardly anyone, this side of the half a dozen or so scholars in the world who read "proto-Akkadian." The Doc, as I soon found out, was never so happy as when he was explaining something to somebody. So he began explaining.

"Proto-Akkadian . . . name of the Underground World . . . the "Great Below" of the Sumerians, *Na-an-Gub* . . . the Babylonians, who came along much later, you know, called it 'Irkalla.' . . ."

"No, I don't think I—"

"Also seems to have been known to the ancient Egyptians and to the Hebrew prophets," he continued, blandly riding over my interjection. "The Hebrews called it *Tehom*, the 'Great Deep' . . . there resided the *nephilim*, the earth-giants of Hebrew myths . . . it appears that the Egyptians may have called the Underground World *Amentet*. It was the Sacred Land, the Underworld of the Dead—the Land in the *West*," he said, with peculiar emphasis, eyes agleam.

"Listen, Professor, I—"

"Now this is particularly interesting, my boy," he rode on, paying me no mind. "For the Sumerians located their own version of Zanthodon—*Na-an-Gub*—in 'the land Martu,' which is to say, in the west."

Tabiz brought us a second round. The Doc knocked his straight back as if it were apple juice instead of pure gin. He licked his lips and continued:

"Even the Moslems know the legend . . . to them it is *Shadukiam*, the underworld of the djinns, ruled by Al-Dimiryat . . . *Also* in the west: "toward the setting sun" . . .

all of these peoples seem to have thought of Zanthodon as a
genuine place; more than one traveler, I hazard, actually
tried to find it . . . none were successful, apparently. As the
Pyramid Texts put it, in one of their more memorable
verses:" and his voice sank to a spooky whisper as he recited,

> "None cometh from thence that he may tell us how they
>   fare,
> That he may tell us what they need, that he may set
>   our hearts at rest,
> Until we also go to the place whither they art gone,
> The place from which there is no returning. . . ."

I have to confess a tingle crawled its way up my spine:
there was a ring to the old boy's voice that the late Boris
Karloff might have envied.

I cleared my throat.

"Underworlds are pretty common in mythology, aren't
they?" I said. "Hell and Hades and Sheol . . ."

He nodded vigorously. "And Duat and Dilmun, *et cetera*
. . . yes, quite right! But as I was saying, my boy—"

He went on; I gave up, leaned back, and savored my cock-
tail. There was no stopping Professor Potter once he got
started talking.

"My first clue as to the whereabouts of the entrance to
Zanthodon I discovered in the old Babylonian creation epic,
Enuma Elish . . . something to the effect that in the month
of Adar, the Door to Irkalla lay 'under the Path of Shimmah.'
. . . Now Shimmah (which the Egyptians called Khonuy)
equates to the sign Pisces; and the month of Adar in the
Babylonian calendar is about the same as the Egyptian month
Mesore. Which means February!"

"Um," I said around a mouthful of martini.

"Then I discovered in Smyrna, in a Greek manuscript of
Zosimus the Panopolitan, reference to a fragment of the old
Egyptian geographer, Claudius Ptolemy (the fragment is considered dubious by some authorities, but there you are! No
one quite agrees on these things)—and Zosimus, quoting
Ptolemy, placed the Mouth of Hades (Ptolemy meant Amentet) beneath the path of Pisces in the month Anthesterion."

He fixed me with an eye glittering with triumph, and a bit
too much gin:

"And the Greek month of Anthesterion is our February!"

I looked at him thoughtfully: "I thought Pisces was a sign of the zodiac," I murmured. "What does 'the Path of Pisces' mean?"

He clucked his tongue, just like a lady math teacher I suffered under in the fifth grade: "The signs of the so-called zodiac are stellar constellations, my boy!" he said reprovingly.

Then, brushing aside the ashtray and the now-empty glasses, he began to trace lines and curves on the tablecloth with the stub of a broken pencil fished from an inner pocket.

"In February," he said breathlessly, "the constellation passes over this belt of North Africa—thus and so—upon this latitude—"

"Latitude 25," I murmured, studying the rude chart he had sketched.

He tapped a bony forefinger on one particular spot.

"Here, I believe."

I mentally reconstructed the location from maps I had seen.

"The Ahaggar Mountains," I said. "In Targa country, surrounded by Tuareg lands. One of the least known, least explored, least visited and most completely inhospitable regions of the entire African continent."

"Precisely."

"And just what do you expect to find there?"

His voice sank to an eerie whisper:

"A hollow mountain, leading to the center of the world."

Chapter 2.

INTO THE AHAGGAR

During the next two weeks I got to know the Professor quite well. His full name—to quote a grubby, thumbprint-smeared visiting card he flashed to overawe customs officials—read:

Professor Percival P. Potter, Ph.D.

He was suspiciously reticent on the question of what that middle initial stood for, but it was on his passport, which I saw by accident.

" 'Penthesileia'?" I read, incredulously.

He fixed me with a frosty, reproving glare.

"You *peeked*."

"Well, I didn't mean to . . . but—*Penthesileia?*"

Professor Potter cleared his throat and gave a little sniff. "My late father was a highly esteemed classical scholar," he informed me coldly. "Penthesileia was the Queen of the Amazons, in an old Roman epic about the Trojan War, by Quintus Smyrnaeus. My father was perhaps overfond of the epic, which is minor and rather florid . . ."

I chuckled. "Your dad was also a bit overfond of alliteration," said I with a grin at Professor Percival Penthesileia Potter, Ph.D.

The Prof was a comical old geezer, all right, but there were a lot of good things you could say about him, as I soon found out. For a skinny little bundle of bones I could pick up in one hand, almost, he had enough guts and courage and boldness for fifty wildcats. During all of our adventures together—and some of them were grueling ordeals, even for a man of my youth—I never once heard him gripe or whimper or complain. He was resourceful, staunch, brave to the point

18

of being foolhardy, and a good man to have at your side when the chips were down.

He was also the smartest guy I've ever known. In fact, he knew more about more things than just about anybody this side of Isaac Asimov. I never did quite figure out just what he was a professor *of*.

For some odd reason, he was rather reticent on that point. Digging around for maps and stuff in the Cairo Museum library, I saw him sight-read a scroll written in old Coptic, and then make a critical remark about the ancient scribe's sloppy use of diacritical marks. Impressive! But his main interest in finding this mountain gate which (presumably) led down into Zanthodon was to search for fossils and minerals. Strolling through another wing of the museum, he rattled off the names (you know, Latin and Greek stuff) of all the dinosaur skeletons we passed.

"What are you, anyway, Doc?" I asked, somewhat baffled. "Here I thought you were a geologist or a mineralogist, and now you're making noises like a—whaddayacallum—fossil hunter, dinosaur expert—"

"Paleontologist?"

"Right: paleontologist," I nodded. "So which is it, anyway?"

He cleared his throat with a little apologetic cough. "Well, a bit of them all, I'm afraid. A bit of a dabbler, you know . . ."

A paleontologist and geologist, who also knows more about ancient Coptic than the old scribes who used to write in it? Well, that was the Prof: a man of parts, as they say.

Later, as I got to know him better, I found out he had equal qualifications in archaeology, ancient languages, and half a dozen other isms and -ologies. Quite a guy!

But I had amused him by being impressed at his scholarly attainments. He chuckled, rather pleased that he had managed to impress me. Which he certainly had—

" '*Un sot toujours un plus sot qui l'admire*,' " he murmured half to himself.

"Come again? That's French, I know, but . . . ?"

"A fool can always find a bigger fool to admire him," he quipped, sardonically.

"Oh, yeah? Who says?"

"Boileau-Despréaux," he replied smugly.

I ground my teeth, cudgeling my memory for a scrap of La Rochefoucauld I half remembered from college:

"Says you," I snorted. " '*Il n'y pas des sots si incommodes que ceux qui ont de l'esprit*'!"

He looked surprised: rather as if a pet chimpanzee had begun a critique of Einstein's math.

" 'There are no fools so troublesome as those who have some wit,' " he translated. "My boy, you delight me! A splendid put-down, and quite apropos. But I wonder if you recall Goethe's pointed remark . . . '*Wir sind gewohnt dass die Menschen verhöhnen was sie nicht verstehen*'?"

"Only thing I ever read by Goethe was *Faust*," I had to admit. His eyes twinkled.

"But it *is* from *Faust*, my dear boy! 'We are used to see that man despises what he never comprehends.' There, I trust that puts you in your place?"

It certainly did.

With all those "p's" in his name, I suppose he just naturally had to be a . . . *polymath.*

The Ahaggar region which was our goal was many hundreds of miles to the west of Port Said; the entire breadth of the African continent stretched between where we were and where we wanted to be.

Well, one thing was sure: I couldn't fly Babe (my affectionate pet-name for the helicopter I had inherited, sort of, from my former partner in crime) all the way there. There's rather a noticeable lack of filling stations in the North Sahara.

We decided to ship the Sikorsky to Morocco by a rusty old tub of a tramp steamer. The nice thing about this was that it wouldn't cost me—or him, rather—one single *pistole*. This was because the fat, fiercely mustached Turk who owned the steamer owed me a favor or three. And *that* was because once upon a time we had both been smuggling guns and ammo into one of those little pepper-pot Middle East wars. *My* side won; his side lost their shirts—and mostly because the ammo he sold them didn't fit the guns he had also peddled to them.

To this day, that particular government would like very much to get their mitts on a fat guy named Kemal Bey. And the favor I could do *him* was to keep my yap shut, while the favor he could do *me* was to carry Babe, the Professor and me down the Mediterranean coast to Morocco. This would not be all that hard to do, since, although Kemal's rusty old tub was hardly much bigger than one of those tugboats they have back in New York Harbor, the chopper could be dismantled and stripped down with a little time, a mite of effort, and a good variety of wrenches.

Kemal Bey groaned and griped and called upon his gods, but relented in the end, and did as I asked. It would take us some weeks to sail down the coast of North Africa, through the Straits and down the west coast past Casablanca to the little seaport town of Agadir, which was smack-dab on the thirtieth parallel, almost.

From that point on, traveling inland, the only thing to do was fly in the chopper, which meant we had to pack along plenty of high octane. This could be procured on the black market in Cairo easily enough, and could be shipped in Kemal's cramped hold. Once we came ashore in Morocco, though, we would have to fly with the gas aboard, which was a mite dangerous.

During our days and nights at sea, I did a lot of thinking about the Prof's scheme. And the more I thought about it, the wackier it seemed. Oh, he was smart enough, but like your typical stereotype of the absent-minded professor, nose buried in books and all, he had about as much practicality as I pack around in the tip of my little finger. Over one of Kemal's lousy dinners—bad fish and raw onions and undrinkable Turkish booze—I asked him the value he estimated for the fossils and rare minerals he hoped to find in the Ahaggar.

"Value, my boy? Dollars-and-cents, you mean? Practically worthless . . . but the value to *science*—"

"I thought so," I groaned.

He looked prim. "I perceive, my boy, that you consider me a science-for-the-sake-of-science fanatic . . . not so at all, I assure you. Fossils are worth little on the open market, that is true, unfortunately; but the region into which we are traveling is known to contain rich fossil beds ranging from the Upper Jurassic to the Lower Cretaceous . . . we can expect to find the remains of brachyosaurus, one of the largest of all the giant saurians, and we can hope for gigantosaurus and perhaps even dichraeosaurus . . . also iguanodonts and even small pterosaurs. When Werner Janensch of the Berlin

Museum excavated in and about those regions back in 1909, he discovered a spectacular skeleton of brachyosaurus and discovered over fifty specimens of kentrurosaurus, an African relative of the stegosaur."

"You've got my head swimming," I confessed. He snorted.

"I assure you, my boy, that a well-preserved and complete skeleton of any of the above reptilia will be an intrinsically valuable find."

"How old is this underground place you hope to discover?" I asked, more to swerve the conversation away from all those jaw-cracking names than from any other motive.

"I believe that Zanthodon was formed in the middle of the Mesozoic, which means it has existed for something like 150,-000,000 years."

One hundred and fifty million years sounded like a lot of years to me, and I said as much. I also pointed out that he said the Ahaggar region abounded in Jurassic and Cretaceous life forms: and now he was talking about the Mesozoic.

He disintegrated me with a look of vitriolic contempt.

"Mighty Mendel, boy, didn't they teach you *anything* at University?" he snapped. "If not, then pray permit me to inform you that the Mesozoic Era began some two hundred million years ago and terminated about seventy million years B.C. It is divided, I will have you understand, into three major subdivisions; and these are known as—taking the earlier period first—the Triassic, which lasted 35,000,000 years, the Jurassic, which was of similar duration, and—lastly—the Cretaceous, which extended for some sixty million years."

"Oh," I said in a small voice. And rapidly changed the subject entirely.

And about time, too.

So I got myself hired to go volcano-hunting and dinosaur-digging. Well, I've had worse jobs, I suppose.

Of course, I could have turned the Professor down flat when he tried to hire me. His wacky scheme sounded dangerous and uncertain from the beginning. But, if you will recall, I had left my last employment with about seventy bucks in my jeans, and by this time, after grubbing around Port Said for a couple of weeks, the exchequer was down to less than fifty. Which wouldn't last long.

To be blunt, I needed a job. Any job.

This fact the Prof figured out back during our first conversation together, when we had drinks at the Cafe Umbala after I rescued him from the two muggers. I had been ordering my meals there for the past two weeks, and when the check came and I tried to coax Tabiz to put the bill on my tab, it turned out to be a bit too heavy already.

"Never mind, my boy," said the Prof grandly. "Ah, waiter . . . can the management of this estimable establishment possibly cash a one hundred dollar bill, perchance?"

The Nubian rolled his eyes widely.

"A hunnahd dollah *Ahmericain?*" he inquired, reverence throbbing in his hushed tones.

"Precisely," sniffed the Prof.

And so I got hired. It seems the Prof had finished up his work for the Egypt Exploration Society and still had a fat wad of greenbacks left over from the sumptuous foundation grant he had wheedled out of the fat cats at his old alma mater. One look at the bankroll he flashed under the table to me, and I was a goner. No matter how wacky his theories might be, or how nutty his ideas were, if he was going to pick up the tab for this expedition into the Back of the Beyond, well, I'm willing to fly him to the gates of hell—and back, if he can pay my bill.

We came ashore at Agadar under a slight drizzle which is rare for these latitudes and this time of year. It took four stevedores to wrestle the 'copter onto the dock, and half the night for the Professor and me to put Babe back together again and get her running smoothly.

By dawn we were fueled up and ready to leave. What with all the petrol tins and food and medical supplies we had packed aboard, it was a wonder the bird could fly at all, but Sikorsky builds 'em tough, and Babe took to the air and wobbled a bit, but stayed aloft.

From Agadar we flew almost directly south, beyond Merijinat and Tagoujalet, taking it by slow and easy stages, landing only to sleep when we had to and eat when we must.

From just beyond Tagoujalet, I turned and flew almost due east . . . following the directions the Professor had calculated from the old maps.

Even under the most ideal conditions, it would take us a couple of days to get to the Ahaggar region, and then maybe a couple of days more to find the mountain the Prof had christened Mount Zanthodon.

Was it actually the entrance to the Underground World the old geographers and myth-makers had written about?

Only time would tell . . .

We flew on . . . into the east; into the rising sun.

And into the Unknown.

Chapter 3.

THE HOLLOW MOUNTAIN

After leaving Tagoujalet, we had some eight hundred miles of Africa to cross by air. Which included some of the worst terrain in all these parts of the Dark Continent: parched desertlands, where the wells and oases were few and far between; stony tundra, where only the hardiest vegetation could manage to subsist; and the domains of the savage, still-untamed Tuareg tribesmen.

And we were heading into an even more forbidding region, which even the fearless Tuaregs shunned.

In the northernmost part of the El Djouf, we flew to Taoudeni, where we took on our last stores and provisions, and filled the water canisters to the brim. From this point on, we would be flying directly east, into the sun, and toward the mountain country.

The highest peak in the Ahaggars is Mount Tahat. At 9,840 feet, it was one of the tallest mountains in all of Africa; and I certainly hoped the mountain the Professor was searching for was nowhere near that height, for Babe simply couldn't fly as high as ten thousand feet. He assured me that *our* mountain was only a fraction of Tahat's height.

It had *better* be, I thought to myself grimly!

Since there was nothing else to do to while away the time our trip consumed, we talked. And got to know each other pretty well. One thing that had been puzzling me was this hollow mountain stuff—and just why the Professor thought there was some sort of a giant cavern world beneath it. So I asked him.

"All those old myths and legends aside, Doc, what makes you think there's a hollow mountain in the Ahaggar anyway, with all that space under it?"

"I have a theory," he said. (The old boy had a theory

25

about nearly everything under the sun, so this didn't surprise me any.)

"So what's your theory?"

He started talking in that precise yet meandering, formal and pedantic way he had, which I was beginning to get used to.

Sometime during the Jurassic Era, or maybe a while before, Professor Potter theorized that the earth had collided with an immense meteorite of contraterrene matter.

"Come again?"

"Contraterrene matter," he repeated. Then, with a little *tut-tut*, "Eternal Einstein, my boy, you must know *something* about physics? . . . Contraterrene matter is the mirror-opposite of ordinary matter . . . where a particle of ordinary, or terrene, matter has a positive charge, a contraterrene particle contains a negative charge, and so on and *vice-versa*. . . ."

"Okay, I got that."

"Well, then . . . it has long been known, or at least theorized, that when the two forms of matter touch, a terrific explosion will result—an explosion of nuclear proportions."

"And how large was this meteor you're talking about?"

He looked owlishly solemn. "Perfectly immense; it is difficult, if not actually impossible, to estimate its full original size from the scanty evidence I have managed to accumulate."

"And when it hit the earth, there would have been a big bang, eh?"

"As you say, my boy, a *very* big bang . . . equal to the blast force of literally *dozens* of hydrogen bombs."

The mental picture conjured up did not exactly make me feel comfortable. "Okay . . . what else?"

His watery blue eyes agleam with enthusiasm, he launched into his spiel. The meteorite, he believed, had struck earth somewhere in the Ahaggar region of North Africa . . . and as far back as we have any records, geographers have reported the crater of an extinct and very ancient volcano in those mountains: Greek merchants and travelers, Roman soldiers and scholars, Victorian explorers and adventurers had all mentioned it, although few of them ever seemed to have actually gotten there, since that was Tuareg country, and the Tuareg tribesmen are not only the best horsemen in North

Africa, but have a well-deserved reputation for inhospitality carried to the point of hostility.

"My astronomer friend, Franklyn, at Hayden Institute, worked out the orbit," he explained excitedly, "and calculated the angle at which the seetee meteorite entered the earth's atmosphere—"

"Seetee?"

"A less-formal term for contraterrene matter . . . please, my boy, if you are not able to keep pace with my disquisition, save your questions until I am through explaining—!"

"And you think it went straight down the cone of the dead volcano?" I hazarded. He blinked surprisedly, as he always did when I said something intelligent.

"Precisely, my boy! And if my calculations are correct, it would have been some hundreds of miles below the earth's crust before the meteor came into contact with normal matter. The explosion would have been of an unprecedented scale of magnitude. Hundreds of thousands of tons of solid rock would have instantly vaporized . . . forming a huge bubble of impacted molten rock far below the planet's surface . . ."

"How huge?" I asked. He shook his head.

"No way of telling, I fear . . . we shall soon see for ourselves."

"That's why you wanted a helicopter!" I said, suddenly putting two and two together and coming up with at least three and nine-tenths.

"Exactly, my boy . . . I plan to descend into the crater of the volcano—let us christen it Mount Zanthodon, and employ the term hereafter as a verbal shortcut."

"Well . . . Babe can do it, I suppose," I muttered dubiously. "Depending on the width of the crater, that is. What do we do if it narrows on us before we get down to the center of the earth?"

"We get out and look about," he said primly, hefting the shiny new geological pick he had purchased in the Cairo market. I groaned and tried to pretend I hadn't heard.

Actually, it wasn't the center of the earth we were going to at all. That was just the Prof's gift for dramatic hyperbole. This side of the fantastic novels of Jules Verne and Edgar Rice Burroughs, nobody is ever going to get that deep into the planet because of the heat of the magma core, if for no other reason. But even a hundred miles down, which was about as deep as Potter reckoned the Underground World to be, was deep enough.

Deeper than any man has ever gone before. . . .

Well, to make a long story just a wee bit shorter, it was there all right—the mountain, I mean. And only a little more than a thousand or so feet high: I hadn't needed to worry about it being anywhere like the height of Mount Tahat, after all.

We made camp on the shoulder of the extinct volcano which the Professor had christened Mount Zanthodon. That put us up above the brush and—theoretically—out of the reach of whatever predators might be roaming around this part of the country. I wrestled with putting up the tent while the Professor twiddled with his instruments, taking measurements and pinpointing the latitude and longitude on his charts with his customary precision.

Then we unloaded everything from the chopper except enough gasoline to get us down to the bottom of the crater's shaft, stashing away our reserve fuel for the return trip to Agadar. Just in case the stories were full of bunk about how the Tuareg tribesmen shunned this area, and to prevent our fuel from being stolen, I hid it by the simple expedient of burying it under the loose, flaky soil which clothed the flanks of the mountain.

With dawn the next day we were to make our first attempt at the descent.

Needless to say, neither of us got much sleep.

We were up early the next morning, for the Professor was hot to get started. My fears about the width of the crater proved groundless, for from lip to lip the crater was more than wide enough to accommodate Babe. Of course, there was no way of knowing in advance how swiftly the shaft might narrow, once we began our descent, and from the top it was impossible to guess.

The Professor puttered about the lip of the crater with something resembling a Geiger. He returned jubilant, reporting that the residual amount of background radiation suggested that his theory was absolutely correct, for the radioactivity was about that which he would expect to find left over from such an underground explosion as he had postulated.

"How dangerous is it?"

"Oh, nothing to worry about at all," he burbled. "In fact, only a special instrument as sensitive as mine could detect it at all . . . no hazard to our health whatsoever!"

I guess I had to be satisfied with that.

And so we started down. At the lip of the crater the width of the central shaft measured about two hundred feet in diameter and roughly six hundred feet in circumference. The great shaft yawned beneath us, seeming to go down and down forever, dwindling into inky darkness. It was a fantastic sight, I must admit; also, a frightening one. But we had not come all this way to sightsee; so I kicked Babe about, centered her above the shaft, and we began the descent.

The sides of the shaft were almost perpendicular, like the sides of a well; but there were jagged outcroppings and protuberances to watch out for, so I guided Babe down carefully, and very slowly, using the special spotlights we had ordered to be installed back at Cairo to illuminate the crater walls.

The sides of the shaft were thickly coated with lava, very porous and crumbling; in the enclosed space, Babe's engine made a deafening racket. Bits and chunks of lava, jarred loose by the noise, went bouncing and ricocheting down. But the Professor reassured me that the dangers of creating a landslide were minute.

Well, he'd been right about everything so far; I would trust him to be right about this fact.

Jaws grimly set, I coaxed Babe down yard by yard. When we were about two hundred feet below the mouth of the crater, darkness closed in, thick and impenetrable, and I was very glad we had thought about installing those spots. Because now we really needed them.

If we so much as nudged against the side of the crater, or hit one of those projecting shelves or spurs of lava which jutted crazily out from the walls, seemingly at random, Babe could snap her rotors. We would still descend, of course, in that case, but a lot more quickly than we wanted to, and our landing would be a bad one.

The Professor was peering with fascination at the rock strata as we sank past the four-hundred-foot point. I suppose any geologist would have been fascinated by what he saw—he yelled, over the roar of the engine, stuff about "combustible carbons," "silurians," and "primordial soil," but I was too busy gritting my teeth to bother listening.

Above our heads the circular opening framed a disc of day, which dwindled to the size of a dime. Now we were entered into the regions of Eternal Night, where light of the sun has but seldom penetrated since the planet was formed. It was an eerie experience, even a thrilling one, to have gone where no human foot had ever gone before us.

I would have traded the thrill for my favorite table at the Cafe Umbala and a good stiff martini and a glimpse of Tabiz's grin.

The glow of a flashlight lit the cabin and broke the gloomy pattern of my thoughts. By its glare, the Professor peered intently at his instruments.

"Two thousand five hundred feet, my boy," he whispered hoarsely. "We are below the very base of Mount Zanthodon at this point . . . in fact, we are beneath the earth's crust!"

I felt a momentary qualm of uneasiness go through me. Then I stiffened my spine and set my jaw firmly.

"How's the radiation count?"

"Still the same amount of background radiation," he murmured. "I do not anticipate that it shall rise to a level even remotely dangerous . . . the radioactivity released by the Jurassic explosion would have fallen to harmless levels many millions of years ago . . . but what of the width of the shaft?"

"Still about the same," I said tersely, estimating with my eye. "Doesn't look as if it's *ever* gonna narrow!"

Nor did it when we reached the depth of a mile, then five miles, then ten.

And so we continued our descent into the regions of Eternal Night and our journey to the Underground World.

Chapter 4.

BENEATH
THE EARTH'S CRUST

At the depth of twenty-five miles the barometric apparatus we had used to measure our depth became thoroughly useless, as the weight of the air in the shaft accumulated beyond that of sea level. We switched over to the manometer, which was inefficient for some reason.

The air, although dense, was still perfectly breathable and even fresh. I suppose the volcanic shaft above us acted as a colossal chimney, drawing the stale cavern air out and replacing it with fresh air from the surface above. The pervading temperature had grown considerably warmer, but certainly not unendurable. We began shedding our outer garments.

At this depth, the lava walls were gorgeously colored, and the coating had formed into swelling blisters very curious to see. Crystals of opaque quartz and veins and splatters of once-liquid glass blazed and glittered awesomely in the light of our lamps. It was a fairyland of dazzling light and color . . . no more gorgeous or fantastic a sight could have met the eyes of Aladdin, when he descended into the caverns of the Wonderful Lamp.

The profuse wealth of minerals must have thrilled the Professor to the core. He jumped up and down in the bucket seat, peering nearsightedly at the wealth of mineral specimens that moved past our view, scribbling feverishly in his little black notebook, making excited comments to me in a high-squeaky voice.

We could no longer accurately measure our depth because of the unexpected failure of the manometer; but about an hour later, when we must have reached a depth of more than thirty miles, we became increasingly aware of a most peculiar phenomenon.

The darkness, which had been as impenetrable as a sea of black ink, began to . . . *lighten.*

At first, we didn't notice it, because we were still descending through a zone of sparkling quartz and streaked glass. The gradual fading of the eternal dark we consigned to the ten thousand flickering, wandering reflections of our spotlights.

But when we had passed below that glittering zone, we could no longer fail to notice the ebbing of the midnight dark of the abyss, and its peculiar dawn-like lightening.

"I wonder if the residual radioactivity could possibly be reacting with chemicals in the rock, causing an effect similar to that of phosphorescence," the Professor mused.

I couldn't say, myself, but was heartily glad for every bit of light I could get. For the shaft had narrowed considerably in the last half-mile, and steering Babe on a safe descent had become increasingly tricky.

At the depth of about thirty-eight miles, the queer, seemingly sourceless light had strengthened almost to the intensity of late afternoon sunlight. We could clearly make out the veins and contours and variegated hues of the mineral strata as we sank past them, even without the use of artificial light.

At about forty-two miles down, we began to notice something else that was every bit as exciting to the professor. Rock-mold and spongy lichens grew in scabrous patches along the fissures in the rock walls of the crater shaft, and we descended past a level shelf-like outcropping covered with fantastic pale-yellow mushrooms a foot high.

"Dear Darwin! Just think of it, my boy," the Professor marvelled in hushed tones. "There is *life* even at this depth within the earth . . . !"

It had grown increasingly warmer until the temperatures within the cabin of the helicopter were swampy and tropical. Sweat poured off us, soaking through our khaki clothing; but the heat was nothing at all like the suffocating warmth I had imagined we would find here beneath the earth's crust.

And the air still smelled fresh and moist.

Although the volcanic shaft narrowed a bit more, somewhere around the depth of sixty or seventy miles beneath the surface, it still afforded sufficient leeway for Babe to continue descending.

I began to wonder if the shaft had any bottom at all, and entertained wild fantasies of flying directly through the earth until we came out the other side! This was sheerest nonsense, of course; but, still and all, it did begin to seem that we could keep on going down into the earth's core forever.

Thankfully, there didn't seem to be much worry about our running out of fuel. I had loaded Babe with subsidiary gas tanks everywhere subsidiary gas tanks could be tied, strapped, bolted or stored aboard the chopper. And this sort of straight-down descent didn't really consume much gas at all.

But after some hours of this, I began to get weary. The nervous tension of inching Babe down, keeping one eye on the walls and the other peeled for unexpected spurs and projections, had begun to wear my strength down.

The Professor volunteered to spell me at the controls while I napped. I taught him exactly what to do and impressed upon him the importance of keeping his mind on what he was doing and ignoring the scenery.

"Leaping Lindbergh, my boy!" he said scoffingly. "I was flying before you were born—"

"Yeah, but not helicopters, I don't think," I retorted rather ungrammatically.

I suppose it was pretty dumb of me to turn the controls over to the living stereotype of the "absent-minded professor," but I was bushed and simply had to get a little shut-eye. And I didn't think anything much could possibly happen: the shaft was still roomy enough to make it easy for a pilot to steer Babe's rotors away from dangerous projections, and the descent was actually a lot easier and less risky now that the peculiar luminosity had increased almost to the strength of daylight.

So I climbed in the back, curled up among the gas tins, pulled my flight jacket over my shoulders, and dozed off.

I awoke with a sudden start when the world turned upside down with a bang and I flew out the cabin door, which had sprung open.

I ended up on my back on a mossy bank, head throbbing to the reverberations of the crash. I looked around wildly, wondering if I was still in my dream.

Whatever it was, this was surely no dream! I have had a

few wild ones in my time, but never a dream to match the likes of this baby. . . .

Above me stretched an oddly luminous sky, with clouds aplenty but no sun in sight.

And the sky was not blue, but a peculiar shade of golden green, like nothing I have ever seen before. I looked up—

And there was a hole in the sky.

It was almost directly overhead. Round and ragged-edged, and blurry, as if the intervening atmosphere were thick with steamy vapors.

Of course, I knew what it was.

The end of the volcanic shaft . . .

I looked down at my feet. My boots were sunk in wet loam. Farther up the slope, thick blue moss grew, starred with fleshy blossoms startlingly colored. Salmon pink and sulphur yellow they were, and they resembled sea anemones more than any flowers I had ever seen.

I raised my eyes.

Babe lay half sunk in the shoulder of the slope, one of her rotors snapped off near the hub, and the rotor-shaft itself still revolving with a *flap-flap* sound. Her plexiglass cabin was severely dented and cracked by collision with the ground, and one of the two cabin doors was dangling open on broken hinges. That must have been the one I was thrown out of.

I looked around.

The chopper had crashed in the slope of a rounded hill near the edge of a wide river or perhaps a lagoon. The water was murky, dull green, and bubbly with froth. The fringe of sand about it was dun colored, littered with pebbles and broken shells and bits of wood. The hill rose behind where Babe had come to rest to greet the margin of a forest. It was a most queer looking forest, indeed, made up of tall, feathery trees which looked like an odd cross between bamboo and willow.

Tree ferns? I thought, my mind spinning crazily.

The forest was a veritable jungle, and the trees seemed rooted in glaucous, slimy mud. Some of the trees seemed familiar enough—hemlocks and cypresses and soaring redwoods—not too much different from the varieties known to me. But other trees were like nothing known to me: there was a very common broad-leafed tree rather resembling a gingko, its little fan-shaped leaves close-set on thick, squirming boughs like the tentacles of an octopus.

The air was steamy, moist and humid. And rank with the odors of the lagoon, stale mud, stagnant water, rotting vegetation. The ground was thick with moss, but I saw nothing in sight resembling ordinary grass or bushes or flowers.

From the slight elevation on which I stood, I could see that the cavern world, if such indeed it was—and such indeed it *was*—was of enormous, virtually unlimited extent.

I could see no horizon; the steamy air thickened, blurring far details. A ragged line of blue-green trees marked a jungle beyond the little lagoon, with dim hills beyond that, and then—vision ended.

I had a sudden crazy hunch that this was a land that time had forgotten—a leftover from the prehistoric past! Memories of Burroughs' Pellucidar, the world at the earth's core, spun dizzily through my brain.

Then the mud stirred and a clumsy shape came shouldering between the tall trees, and I stared into a grinning, lipless mouth lined with bristling fangs.

And the world went mad.

The thing was only, I suppose, about three or four feet long; but, then, so's a king cobra. It was squat and bowlegged and built low to the ground and it walked with an odd, lurching waddle of a gait because its hind legs were longer than its forelegs. It was a mossy dark green all over its warty, armored hide, except in throat and belly, where the color paled to a muddy yellow. It had two rows of bony plates down its back and along the length of its thick, alligator-like tail.

But its head wasn't much like an alligator's, being neckless and snubby in the snout. Under bony brows, its eyes were unwinking pits of bright ferocity, unnervingly scarlet. When it grinned, both jaws proved lined with sharp white fangs longer than my fingers.

There were an awful lot of them, those fangs. . . .

It gave me a long, unwinking gaze, then waddled around behind the wrecked helicopter. I heard a pounce, a squeal; and it emerged into view chewing on something that dribbled raw crimson down its pulsing throat.

And quick fear welled up within me—

"Professor!" I squawked, grabbing at my hip with shaking

fingers, trying to fumble open the snap on the holster strapped to my waist, where a well-oiled .45 reposed.

I ran around to the other side of the chopper, and stopped so suddenly a viewer might have thought I had collided with an invisible wall. For there he stood, sun helmet askew, pince-nez tilted to one side, a bruise on his cheekbone, but otherwise (as far as I could see) all in one piece. He stared after the reptile as it waddled unhurriedly away to finish its meal.

"Eh? What, my boy?"

"Just wanted to make sure that wasn't a piece of you that pint-sized croc was nibbling," I breathed, woozy with relief.

In his rapt, entranced state he scarcely heard me.

"Oh, by Linnaeus, Lamarck and Lydekker, my boy, isn't it purely *wonderful*," he murmured dreamily, gazing after the retreating reptile.

"Ugliest damn croc I ever saw," I said rudely. He blinked vaguely.

"Eh, my boy? . . . Yes, you're right . . . well, it is not exactly a true crocodile, but close enough, close enough . . . give the poor creature another thirty million years or so, and it will evolve into your true and genuine *Crocodylus niloticus* . . . unless, of course, evolution and its forces have been suspended here, as I more than half suspect to be the case . . . how beautiful!" he sighed, staring after the repulsive creature.

"Beautiful?" I repeated, with a snort. "All depends on taste, I suppose. Give me Ursula Andress in a bikini, and you can keep all the dwarf crocs in the world . . ."

But he was paying no attention to me, staring after the reptile. "Protosuchus," he whispered, "as I live and breathe! . . . and hitherto found only in Triassic strata in Arizona . . . a descendant of the phytosaurs . . . utterly remarkable!"

"You mean that was a *dinosaur*?" I demanded, my voice rising into a squeak at the end.

"Yes, my boy," he said dreamily, "that was certainly a dinosaur."

Welcome to Zanthodon, I thought to myself, feebly.

Part Two

THE
UNDERGROUND WORLD

Chapter 5.

LAND OF MONSTERS

Now that my fears concerning the Professor's safety were relieved, we had time to compare notes. It seems that the helicopter had emerged so suddenly into the vast open space, that it had taken Potter quite by surprise.

As I had not instructed him how to land the chopper—there being no particular reason to teach him that—he did the best he could in the few moments available to him.

We checked out Babe, and she was a sorry sight. Although not as much a total loss as she would have been had the gas tanks exploded, she was still a long ways from being airworthy. One rotor blade was snapped off short; another was bent. We would require the services of a blacksmith in setting that part of the damage to right. And where, in all of this incredible cavern-world, could we expect to find a smithy?

The Professor—predictably—was fascinated by his discovery. While I peered and poked and pried at the undercarriage, trying to ascertain the extent of the damage, he stared about him in dazzled wonder.

"Incredible, my boy, simply incredible!" he breathed enthusiastically. "Zanthodon is even more miraculous than I had dreamed . . . those trees over there are Jurassic conifers, extinct in the upper world for untold ages."

"Yeah? And what are those feathery bamboo-type things?" I grunted, nodding at the tall growths which fringed the lagoon.

"Cycads, my boy . . . tree-ferns, likewise extinct. Utterly marvelous: a paleontologist's dream come true!"

He had expected to find some interesting fossils, so I can readily understand his excitement at finding them alive and well, flourishing here beneath the earth's crust where the temperature was humid, subtropical, and—above all—*stable*.

"Did you expect this place to be so big?" I inquired, rising

39

to my feet and dusting off my knees. He shook his head, sun helmet wobbling.

"Not precisely . . . I estimate the cavern-world as being about five hundred miles by five hundred, almost perfectly circular," he mused. That didn't sound like so much to me, and I said so.

He snorted. "That means Zanthodon consists of *a quarter of a million* square miles, my boy."

"That much?"

"That much!"

"Well, we're stuck here for a while, at least," I said grimly. "Babe can't fly until we repair her rotors—*yow!*"

I yelled, ducked, hit the dirt—and the Professor was not far behind me.

"What was *that*?" I gasped, as the enormous kite-shaped black shadow sailed on over the lagoon. Glancing up, I saw wide, bat-like membranous wings, a long snaky head and tail, and a beaklike muzzle filled with an incredible number of *very* long teeth.

"Either a pteranodon or perhaps a true pterodactyl," murmured the Professor abstractedly, peering at the soaring reptile. "How remarkable that here life forms otherwise extinct still flourish . . . no pteranodon has flown the skies of the upper world for seventy million years and more, yet here they seem to thrive, if yonder specimen is indicative . . ."

"Yeah," I grunted, staring after the winged monster as it lazily flapped away over the treetops. "And come to think of it, Doc, how'd 'you suppose the dinosaurs *got* down here, anyway? That volcano crater is straight down for miles and miles. Maybe a flying critter like that one that just went by could have gotten here under his own steam, but the protocroc we saw a minute ago certainly couldn't."

He frowned, rubbing his brow with a grubby forefinger. "There may well be, probably are, other entrances to Zanthodon besides the one by which we traveled here . . . side vents, volcano fumaroles . . . and some of them may perhaps descend into the cavern-world at an angle less steep, thus affording passage to the four-footed saurians."

Warming to his latest theory, the Professor began a rambling discourse that was more like thinking out loud than anything else. No one quite knows what killed the dinosaurs off, but the difficulty of obtaining sufficient food, climactic changes to which the cold-blooded reptiles could not comfortably adjust, all these probably share the blame. He made it seem very understandable that some of the saurians, drifting down across Europe in search of food or warmer climes, might have crossed the Gibralter land-bridge (for in those ages, the Mediterranean was only a land-locked lake), finding their way to North Africa and, some of them, into Zanthodon.

His explanation sounded pretty reasonable to me, but then, I'm no scientist.

"Just think of it, my boy," he breathed, eyes agleam with the good old scientific fervor, "living survivors of a lost age, dwelling here beneath the earth's crust . . . ah, Holy Huxley and Dear Darwin! When we return again to the upper world, we shall astound the entire scientific community—or we could, that is; *especially* if we were to bring back *a living specimen* of a species known to have perished into extinction scores of millions of years ago! . . . Why, think of it!—Mighty Mendel, but it could make our names forever undying and immortal in the annals of exploration and discovery . . . !"

I could just imagine trying to cram several hundred pounds of fanged fury into Babe's cramped little cabin, but I said nothing. No reason to shatter the Professor's dream.

"*If* we get back," I couldn't resist pointing out. "The way things stand right now, Babe's in no condition to handle that ascent. I couldn't even get her off the ground, lacking those rotor-blades."

He rubbed his hands together briskly, glancing around.

"Then we shall begin work at once," he puffed. "We'll make camp on that high ground . . . and we must find a source of fresh water, as I presume the lagoon is salty . . . some manner of rude palisade should keep the larger predators at bay while we effect repairs on your machine. Let me see, now . . . we can make charcoal with some of the dry wood from the jungle, build an oven with loose rocks, rig up some sort of smithy using spare parts from your tool box . . . the repairs will be crude, certainly, and only temporary, but surely with your strength and my skill, we can render the machine airworthy again within a matter of weeks—perhaps even days."

"I suppose so," I said, a bit dubious about the whole thing.

"But the main problem is going to be keeping ourselves alive
that long."

And that *was* going to be a problem!

The only weapon I had thought to bring along was my .45,
for which I had plenty of ammo. But the automatic was not
going to be much good against any of the bigger dinosaurs,
and the Professor and I both knew it. What we needed for
that was a good, huge elephant gun. If not a mortar!

If I had known we were going to be marooned here, like
characters out of *King Kong* or *The Lost World*, I could
have bought some more sophisticated weaponry on the black
market back in Cairo. A beltfull of fragmentation grenades
would certainly come in handy, I thought to myself wistfully.
The Professor pooh-poohed my fears.

"Cease your trepidations, my boy," he huffed. "Most of the
giant saurians are vegetarians, and no more dangerous than
milk cattle . . . now let us begin looking for a source of
fresh water."

I thought to myself of a prize bull that had gored a careless farmhand to death back home when I had been a kid,
but decided not to mention it. The Professor was a hard guy
to argue with. He always had fifty-seven reasons why he was
right and I was wrong, and I had to agree that he certainly
knew more about dinosaurs than I did.

So we started out, searching for a spring. In order not to
get ourselves lost, we decided to trace an ever-widening
circle, using the site of Babe's wreck as the center of the spi-
ral. Just in case we did run into trouble, I insisted on taking
along a light backpack of medical supplies and food. He
grumbled that this was an unnecessary precaution, but relented and gave me my head in the matter.

Under the steamy skies of Zanthodon's perpetual day we
started off. The Professor had a theory about the uncanny
daylight which bathed the jungle country beneath the earth:
he figured that the original explosion which had created the
Underground World had reacted chemically with minerals in
the vaporized rock to create an effect not dissimilar to chemi-
cal photoluminescence. He was probably right about this, for
during all the time I was to spend here in Zanthodon the light
never changed or faded or dimmed.

Strange, strange! . . . This world of eternal day where

monsters from the prehistoric past roamed and raged amid jungles left over from Time's forgotten dawn. . . .

But there were even stranger marvels yet to come.

The first inkling we had that we were in serious trouble came swiftly.

A black shadow blotted out the sky and as we threw ourselves prone, there descended on flapping wings like those of a monstrous bat another of those ghastly winged reptiles we had seen earlier.

It was about the size of last year's Buick, its lean and sinewy body covered with leathery, pebbled hide rather than scales, and it had the same long beaklike snout filled with an amazing number of long, sharp, white teeth.

The thing pounced down upon us like a chicken hawk on a couple of fat pullets, clawed feet reaching for our flesh as it fell. I felt a blast of hot, stinking breath and looked up into mad, hungry scarlet eyes—

Then I hit the dirt, rolled, snapped up, leveling my .45. I pumped two slugs into the pterodactyl as it scrabbled about in the mud, trying to get ahold of the Professor. The stench of gunpowder stung my nostrils and the explosion of the gunshots was deafening. The thing squawked, red blood spurted from one wing, and it fell over on its side, clawing at the ground as I dragged the Professor clear, tugging one leg.

"Th-thank you, my b-boy," he panted. "That was a narrow shave . . . henceforward we must keep on the alert for such flying monsters—"

The underbrush rustled as something big and greenish-brown came pushing through. It was bigger than three oxen, with a head the size of an oil-drum. Its cruelly beaked snout bore a short, curved horn thicker than my thigh, and there was nothing but fierce hunger in its little pig-eyes. It looked like the granddaddy of all rhinos, and it came thundering down upon us like a runaway locomotive.

We sprang clear as it crashed into the crippled pterodactyl and sank that nasal horn to the hilt in the bat-bird's leathery chest. It began to crunch and munch juicily, ripping off raw steaks, blood squirting all over; and it was one ugly customer, let me tell you! It stood about seven feet high and was about twenty feet long, and it must have weighed in at two or three tons. It had four squat legs, bowed out at the knees, and a huge, swaying paunch, and a thick tail like an alligator. The thing's feet looked like those of an elephant.

"What the hell is it?" I whispered to the Professor as we took hasty refuge in the bushes.

"I don't precisely know, my boy," he panted. "Obviously a ceratopsian, perhaps a genuine triceratops, I don't know . . ."

"*You* don't know?"

He glared at me with some asperity.

"My boy, there are more than a dozen genera of ceratopsians, and I can't be expected to recognize one at a glance! They look very different, you know, from their skeletons . . . but from the bony shield covering the monster's neck, I should certainly say triceratops . . . but that is very interesting, *very* interesting indeed! For triceratops is known mostly from fossils found in North America—in the state of Montana, to be precise, where I believe the first skulls were discovered in 1888."

"Well, what's it doing here in Africa?" I wanted to know.

He shrugged helplessly. "My boy, your guess is every bit as good as mine!"

"I think we'd better find a tree to climb," I suggested. "That triceratops of yours is just about finished with his pterodactyl snack, and may require something more substantial for the main course—like you and me."

We found a huge, gnarly tree and climbed it. And not a minute too soon . . .

Twenty minutes later we were still sitting there on a tree limb as the monster prowled with ponderous, earth-shaking steps around and around the tree, pausing from time to time to look up at us and grin, showing a vast pair of jaws and a mighty empty looking gullet. The thing's head was at least seven feet from the base of that bony shield to the beaked snout, and looked fully capable of gobbling up both of us at one gulp.

And it didn't look like it was getting bored waiting for lunch, either.

I gave the Professor a look.

"Mostly vegetarians, eh?" I said sarcastically.

Looking remarkably unhappy, the Professor made no comment.

Chapter 6.

BATTLE OF THE GIANTS

Before long it began to rain, which didn't make the Professor any happier. He seemed to hate getting wet as much as any cat, and fussed and fumed as we sat there, treed by a triceratops, getting soaked to the skin in a warm drizzle. The shower, unfortunately, did not seem to dampen the enthusiasm of the lumbering monstrosity below, or diminish his appetite.

I said something to that effect, and the Professor snapped at me waspishly.

"The giant reptiles have very small brains, and the creature will lose interest before long and wander off, having forgotten what he was after in the first place," he said brusquely.

Like most of the Professor's predictions, this one proved to be wrong, too. For, half an hour later, the brute was still lumbering about beneath our perch, and he was beginning to get impatient, too. This impatience took the form of giving the tree we were in a nudge or two with his horned snout. And let me tell you, three tons of armor-plated super-rhino can really nudge! He shook the tree as easily as a housemaid shakes out a feather duster, and we had to hang on for dear life.

"Goodness, but I wish he would stop that infernal shaking!" wheezed the Professor, hugging the rough trunk in his skinny arms. "And if only he would go away—I am far too old for these acrobatics!"

Then followed one of the most ludicrous scenes I have ever witnessed. For, whipping off his sun helmet, to which he had tenaciously clung all this while, he began flapping it at the triceratops below like a man trying to drive away an annoying mosquito.

"Shoo, you nasty thing!—Go away!—Leave us alone, now!—We have no time for this nonsense—Shoo!" he shrilled in an exasperated tone of voice. The monster craned its neck skyward, blinking those tiny piggish eyes at the small, scrawny man above.

I began to laugh so hard I nearly fell off my branch, for the expression on the triceratops' face (or what passed for its face, at least) seemed to me one of blank bafflement. Oh, sure, I know the monster's leathery visage was incapable of displaying any expression, but that's what it looked like to me. It was as if the brute was reacting to a novel experience: for, surely, not too many triceratopses in this day and age have ever been angrily "shooed" by a short-tempered professor!

Our salvation arrived right on schedule, shortly after the shooing. And it took a quite unexpected form. . . .

Vegetation crackled, branches snapped and crunched, as a second huge form came lumbering out of the jungle. I took one look and let my jaw drop down to about here: for I had expected another dinosaur, from all the noise, but what emerged into view was a very big elephant wearing a fur coat!

Our visitor was easily twice the size of any elephant I have ever seen, and entirely covered with a long and wavy blanket of coarse red hair. From beneath its long, prehensile trunk sprouted two fantastic ivory tusks, each a good twelve feet long, and these were extravagantly curled.

I exchanged a look with the Professor, and he was as glazed of eye and dangly of jaw as I.

"But this is utterly impossible . . ." he whispered, half to himself. "A wooly mammoth from the Ice Age! . . . How could it possibly coexist with one of the great carnosaurs?"

"What do you mean?" I asked.

"Why, the mammoths date from the Pleistocene, only one or two million years ago, and the triceratops is a Mesozoic reptile! . . . the two monsters come from ages nearly one hundred and fifty million years apart. . . . This is utterly *fantastic!*"

And what followed was even more fantastic: a duel to the death between hyper-elephant and super-rhino.

Upon spying the dinosaur, the enormous mammoth stopped short. Flapping his ears he lifted his long trunk, giving voice to an enraged squeal of ear-ripping intensity, like a steam whistle gone mad. I got a hunch that this was Jumbo's personal hunting ground, and that the triceratops was intruding where he was not welcome.

As for the dinosaur, he was in a furious temper, anyway, from his frustration at not yet being able to shake down the lunch he had treed. Squaring off, pawing the mud with one enormous forefoot, he lowered his head, aimed that thick, stubby, pointed horn—and charged!

He caught the mammoth right below the knee, goring him deeply. With a scream of pain and fury, the hairy brute went down on all fours with a thump that shook the ground. Then, swinging its huge head from side to side, the mammoth caught the triceratops across one beefy shoulder with the point of his curlicue tusks, ripping open a long-jagged gash between two plates of the reptile's armor.

Honking furiously, the dinosaur backed off, snorting and pawing the mud, gathering his energies for another charge. The mammoth climbed to his feet again, slightly favoring his gored leg.

The two monsters charged at each other, and when they met it was like two armored tanks colliding. The impact was terrific, but neither monster seemed even slightly dazed. And in the next instant they were at it fast and furious, goring with their tusks, trying to knock each other flat with those heavy hammerlike heads. The ground quaked and trees shook to the fury of their battle. It was an awesome spectacle, and the Professor was utterly enthralled.

"Precious Pliny! Think of it, my boy, we are witnessing a combat no human eyes could ever have looked on before in all of the world's history . . . such a duel of prehistoric titans as could only occur here in Zanthodon! Two gigantic monsters from the far ends of time, one a survival from the dim and misty Mesozoic dawn, the other a creature from the Ice Ages, separated from each other by a hundred and fifty million years of evolution . . . incredible!"

I could understand his amazement; back home I have a friend who plays war games with miniature armies, and one of his favorite hobbies is to pit the great generals of history, divided by centuries, against each other: Napoleon against Peter the Great, or Alexander of Macedon against Hannibal, or Julius Caesar against Genghis Khan. My friend Scott would certainly have savored the rare spectacle we witnessed in that unforgettable battle between two titans from Time's remotest dawn!

It wasn't long before I discovered something unexpected and even curious about the fight to which we were the only witnesses. And that is, it was really quite a one-sided contest.

Rather to my surprise, it did seem that the triceratops was getting the worst of it all. I suppose that I was accustomed to thinking of the gigantic prehistoric dinosaurs as colossal monsters, virtually invulnerable—a habit I probably picked up from watching Godzilla movies—but now that I think back on that fantastic battle of maddened giants from the remote past, I have to remember that the mammoth was far bigger and lots heavier than the dinosaur, who was, after all, only about twenty or twenty-five feet long and who must have weighed no more than two or three tons at the most.

Well, the wooly mammoth was about seventeen feet high at the shoulder, and would probably have tipped the scales at two or even three times the triceratops' tonnage. And his legs were like the trunks of the giant redwoods of California; when, after some trying, he finally got the triceratops under one of his legs, and had a chance to set his foot down upon the hapless reptile, he broke its back with a grisly snap that was sickeningly audible.

It was all over quite soon: streaming blood from a half-a-dozen places in his flanks where the triceratops had gored him, the furious mammoth trampled the crippled dinosaur into bloody slime.

And it suddenly occurred to me that this was our cue to make a hasty exit before the victor returned to the tree for the spoils. With his height, and that long trunk, the mammoth could pluck us from the bough as easily as an apple-picker plucks ripe fruit from the branch. I said as much to the Professor, and he chuckled nastily, as he often did when I displayed my ignorance.

"We have little to fear from the mammoth, my boy—although were we to get underfoot, he could make short work of us . . . but, at any rate, we need not fear the beast will attempt to eat us . . . for, unlike the triceratops, the wooly mammoth is a vegetarian like his remote descendant, the elephant."

"Oh," I said. "Well, what do you say we get out of this

tree, anyway? I'd rather like to make tracks out of here while he's still busy making strawberry jam out of the dino."

"Not a bad idea, my boy."

We climbed down out of the tree with a lot more difficulty than we had when going up it, because being chased by a hungry triceratops does tend to improve one's agility. But we got down, anyway, and without attracting any attention from the infuriated mammoth.

"Which way?" I muttered, looking about. With all the excitement, I had lost track of the direction from which we had come.

"That way, I think," whispered the Professor, pointing off to a grove of tree-sized ferns.

About a half an hour later, we sat down on a rotting log to catch our breath, and had to admit to ourselves that we were thoroughly lost. It is peculiarly difficult to tell your direction in a place that has no sun to tell you east from west; but, still, as I sourly remarked to the Professor, I *could* have been smart enough to bring a pocket-compass along.

"Please don't castigate yourself on that omission, my boy," he panted, fanning himself with the sun helmet. "In the first place, I rather doubt if a compass would work at this depth, and in the second. . . ."

But Professor Potter never got a chance to finish his statement, and I never did find out his second reason why I shouldn't blame myself for forgetting to bring along the compass.

For just then the long reeds before us parted, and there shouldered into view the ugliest monstrosity I had yet seen in Zanthodon.

It had a small, flat-browed, wicked little head at the end of a thick, short neck, and it waddled out of the underbrush on four fat legs. The weirdest thing about it was that it was completely armored all over—in bands, like an armadillo. And these tough plates of horny armor were pebbled with hideous wartlike encrustations.

They were also packed bristling with short, blunt spikes. From stem to stern: from the forehead (such as it was) down to the tail—and what a tail! It was shaped like the business end of a giant's club, and boasted two enormous spikes. Since the waddling monstrosity rather looked to weigh a ton or more, I had a feeling that tail could total a Volkswagen with one good swipe.

And it was coming straight at us—

The Professor paled, and uttered a stifled shriek.

As for me, I did a damnfool thing: I whipped out my .45 and put a slug right between its mean little eyes!

Chapter 7.

CASTAWAYS IN YESTERDAY

Which did about as much good as pumping a shot into an oncoming locomotive. The immense reptile with the spiked, warty hide like an overgrown horned toad kept coming, not even wincing as the slug from my automatic slammed into it. Either the slug flattened upon impact or glanced off like a bullet ricocheting from steel plate . . . anyway, it didn't even nick the monster's horny hide.

"C'mon, Doc!" I yelled, jerking the old man to his feet and propelling him before me. We plunged into the reeds at breakneck speed. With that ton of beef to drag along, it didn't look to me as if our club-tailed friend was exactly built for speed. And I figured we could outdistance him, with just a little luck.

But we ran out of luck—and land—at just about the same time.

That is, the jungle through which we were plunging suddenly gave way to pure, oozy swamp. I stopped short, ankle-deep in yellow mud, and grabbed the Professor by one skinny arm just as he was about to plunge into the muck up to his middle.

"We can't run through that, Doc," I panted. "Looks like quicksand to me—quick, the other way!"

But even as we turned to take another route and skirt the swampy area, the ground trembled beneath a ponderous tread and that immense, blunt-nosed, flat-browed head came poking through the brush. The dino had been able to move much quicker than I had thought possible.

I unlimbered my automatic again, feeling trapped and helpless. If one slug hadn't even dented his warty hide, what good was a clipful of bullets? Right then and there, I could have written a five-year mortgage on a large chunk of my soul for one good big elephant gun.

The huge reptile came lumbering down to the shore of the swamp where we stood cornered with our backs to a lake of stinking mud.

Then it reached forward delicately and selected a mawfull of tender reeds which grew along the edge of the marsh. One chomp and it pulled up a half-bushel of reeds in its jaws.

And, with one dull, sleepy eye fixed indifferently upon the two of us, jaws rolling rhythmically like some enormous cow, it began chewing its reed salad.

I let out my breath with a *whoosh*; beside me, the Professor essayed a shaky laugh.

"Ahem! Ah, my boy, if I had only identified the creature a bit earlier, we could have avoided our precipitous flight," he wheezed, climbing out of the muck on wobbly knees.

"What's *that* mean?" I demanded.

"It means that I have been able to identify the creature," he smiled. "From its appearance, it is clearly some genera of ankylosaur . . . I believe it to be a true scolosaurus from the Late Cretaceous . . . like so many of its kind—"

"—A harmless vegetarian?" I finished, sarcastically. He had the grace to blush just a little.

"Just so," he said feebly.

We climbed back up to higher ground, circling the placid grass-eater as it mechanically munched its cud, glancing with an idle and disinterested eye as we passed.

By now we were quite thoroughly lost. I cannot emphasize enough the peculiar difficulty—in fact, the utter impossibility—of finding your way about in a world that has no sun in its sky. Under the steamy skies of Zanthodon, where a perpetual and unwavering noon reigned, there was no slightest hint as to which way was north, south, east or west.

We might be fifty yards from the helicopter, or fifty miles. (Well, not quite that much: we couldn't possibly have come so far in so short a time, but you get the idea.)

We decided simply to keep going until we found either food or water—if not both—or the chopper. I was getting pretty depressed about then, what with being hungry, tired, thirsty, and splattered with mud halfway up to my armpits. Mud squelched glutinously in my boots with every step I took, and my clothes were still wet clear through from that warm shower we had sat through when the triceratops had us treed. And there are few things this side of actual torture or toothaches more uncomfortable than being forced to walk about for long in soaking wet clothes.

Zanthodon is a world of tropic warmth, but, lacking true sunlight; if you get wet it's curiously hard to get dry again, due to the steamy humidity. Not at all the place I'd pick for a winter vacation: as far as I have yet been able to discern, there are no seasons here, and only one climate. Some of those hare-brained weather forecasters who litter the nightly news on television would certainly have a cushy job down here: *Hot, humid, scattered showers and occasional volcanic eruptions* . . . that would do for a good yearful of forecasts!

The Professor was a man of irrepressible enthusiasms, however; you could not keep him gloomy for long, not in a place like this, when everywhere he happened to look he spotted something or other that was (according to him) of unique scientific interest.

"Fascinating, my boy, utterly fascinating," he burbled, jouncing along at my side as we trekked through the jungle.

"What is it now?" I sighed.

"The varieties of flora we have thus far encountered," he said. "Perhaps I should have guessed as much from the variety of fauna we have already met with . . . you recall I remarked a while earlier that something like one hundred and fifty million years separated triceratops from the wooly mammoths of the Ice age . . . ?"

"Yeah, I remember," I said laconically.

"Well, do you notice anything different about this part of the jungle?"

I glanced around. We were tramping through a rather sparse growth of jungle at the time. Around us were things that looked like palm trees, but which had crosshatched, spiny trunks resembling the outsides of pineapples; and what looked like evergreen bushes, eye-high skinny Christmas trees; and tall, fronded, droopy-looking trees. Some of these grew about forty feet high, and there was hardly anything in the way of underbrush.

The Professor was right: this part of the jungle *did* look kind of different . . . so I said as much.

"Pre*cise*ly, young man!" he cackled jubilantly. "When we

first arrived in Zanthodon, we found ourselves in a jungle landscape quite definitely situated in the Early Cretaceous, what with its typical flora of palmlike cycads and tree ferns, and the ancestors of the modern evergreen and gingko . . ."

I recalled the landscape in which we had first found ourselves, and nodded, if only to keep the old boy happy. For he was never so much in his element as when lecturing somebody about something. It is, I understand, an occupational disease of scholars and scientists.

"Well," he continued in a sprightly tone of voice, "we now find ourselves in a landscape decorated with vegetation distinctly Devonian."

"Yeah?" I grunted. "Listen, Doc, these names don't actually mean all that much to me, you know?"

He sniffed reprovingly.

"The Cretaceous began about one hundred and thirty million years ago," he informed me. "But the Devonian is vastly earlier . . . three hundred million years ago, at least."

I glanced around me at the peculiar trees.

"And this stuff is Devonian, eh?"

"Quite indubitably . . . those are aneurophytons over there, a variety of seed fern . . . and those odd-looking bushes are a variety of horsetail called calamites . . ."

"What about those funny-looking trees over there?" I asked, nodding at something that looked as if it had grown from a few seeds dropped down from Mars.

"Archaeosigillaria, a true lycopod, commonly known as club-mosses," he said dreamily. "And these pallid, slender-fronded growths through which we are at the moment strolling are psilophyton, a very primitive form of plant life."

His gaze became ecstatic. "Think of the marvel of it all . . . these very earliest forms of vegetable life died out and became extinct long before the first mammalian brain sluggishly stirred toward a spark of sentience . . . hitherto we have only known them from their fossilized traces or remains—but to actually *look* upon the living plants themselves! Noble Newton!"

I did not exactly share his excited fervor, but I could understand it, I suppose.

"It's like as if we had a Time Machine," I mused, "and had gotten lost in the prehistoric past . . ."

"Precisely so," he sighed. "Castaways of time, marooned in

a forgotten yesterday countless millions of years before our own modern age. . . ."

Just then I took a false step and went to my knees in yellow muck, and rose dripping and foul.

"Very poetic," I grumbled, "but give me the sidewalks of Cairo, or a good filet mignon on Park Avenue."

"My boy," he sighed, "you have no soul!"

"I got plenty of soul, Doc!" I protested. "It's just that I would be enjoying this time trek a lot more if I had brought along a motorcycle. Or a good dry canoe," I added grimly. For we had come to the shore of another lake of watery mud, and it looked like a long walk around it.

Poetry is all very well, and I have nothing against souls, either, for that matter.

But I hate wet clothes and a bootfull of squishy mud can ruin my whole morning!

Chapter 8.

THE SEA
THAT TIME FORGOT

Since there were no dawns or sunsets here in the Underground World, we were going to have to get used to sleeping in the broad daylight of Zanthodon's perpetual noon.

After some hours of weaving through the Devonian jungle, and going around ever-larger and muckier areas of swamp, we were both bone-weary and mighty hungry.

I brought down a small, plump critter that looked like a large lizard walking on its hind legs, planting one slug from my .45 right behind the shoulder. It went down, kicking and twitching, its jaws opening and closing spasmodically, long after its eyes had glazed over and gone dead.

The Professor identified it as a harmless coelurosaur, but you could have fooled me. It was about a yard long and looked very lizardlike to my eye, except that its hind legs were much bigger and more developed than its tiny forelimbs, and it walked erect with a springy, long stride, rather like an ostrich. As it bopped along, it kept bobbing its head back and forth, for all the world like an ordinary pigeon.

"Harmless?" I asked the Professor in a stage whisper—for a yard long is plenty long enough for something to take a chunk out of you. He shrugged.

"Harmless enough . . . a coelurosaur is a scavenger, an eater of dead things . . . no more dangerous than a vulture, and with similar tastes in nutrition."

I wasn't about to debate how dangerous vultures can or cannot be, although I remember a grisly tussle I had with a couple of the ugly birds in the Kalihari Desert (they insisted I was dead, and thus fair game; I insisted I was alive . . . I won).

"Harmless, then?" I repeated, unlimbering my shootin'
iron.

"Harmless."

"Dinner," I said succinctly, and pumped a slug into the
little dinosaur. It expired, twitching, taking about as long to
die as a snake does. With brains as small as most dinos are
supposed to have, it must have taken quite a while for the
notion that it was deceased to have penetrated that small,
hard skull.

I could swear that it was still twitching, even after I had
chopped it up and was roasting the more tender bits of it
over a fire.

And thus it was we ate our first true meal in Zanthodon,
living off the landscape in the approved pioneer manner.

And—incidentally—became the first humans on record to
enjoy dinosaur steak. (Tough, and a little gamy; but not all
that bad!)

Getting to sleep in what could easily pass for broad daylight was another matter entirely. After we had chewed and
swallowed as much of filet of coelurosaur as could be expected of us, we drank and washed our hands from a small bub-
bling spring which gushed from a pile of rocks, and started
looking around for a safe place to sleep.

And learned there really are no safe places to sleep here in
Zanthodon.

I knew this for a fact the third time I fished a wriggling
nine-inch horned proto-lizard out of my bed of grasses.

We gave up the dry land and settled for a perch in a tree.
And at that we had to tie ourselves to the trunk and sleep sitting up, straddling a branch between our legs.

I was so sleepy by that time that I just figured that anything smart or agile enough to climb the tree to get at us was
welcome to the meal. Hell, a man has got to sleep once in a
while . . . and it had certainly been a long and busy day.

I have no idea how long I slept—and I refuse to bore you
by repeating all that stuff about no sun in the sky and so
on—but whenever it was that I did wake up, I was stiff and
sore in every muscle, and had a king-size headache and a
mouth that tasted as if a particularly nasty little furry animal
had decided a few weeks ago to hibernate therein.

By the time I climbed down stiffly from the tree, I discovered muscles in places I had never known I had muscles. Since I am, by comparison, young and fairly limber, you can imagine how Professor Potter felt.

And not having a steaming hot mug of black coffee to wash down our breakfast of cold, greasy coelurosaur leftovers did nothing to improve our dispositions, I assure you. Still and all, the life in the great outdoors is supposed to be hearty and bracing, and also good for you. Maybe it is: it just takes a little getting used to.

We continued our trek through the Devonian jungle. And by this time I was getting pretty damn sick of that Devonian jungle. My idea of jungle comes from watching Tarzan movies, and I feel cheated without lots of jungle vines and exotic, flowering bushes and long grasses and stuff . . . and apparently, grasses, bushes and flowers just plain weren't around during the Devonian.

We kept on going until we could go no farther.

We had run into a sea.

We came to the edge of a bluff, and there before us stretched a vast, seemingly endless expanse of water. Oily waves heaved sluggishly under misty skies, and the glimmering slimy tides broke with a slow, pounding rhythm against fanged barriers of lava rock thickly encrusted with sea growths. The sea expanded before us, stretching to the dim horizon, losing itself in the steamy fogs which hung low over the heaving rollers.

"It is like the first sea, on the very morning of Creation itself," breathed the Professor, clasping his bony hands together in poetic exaltation. And I have to admit it certainly was. His expression became dreamy, as he repeated the old, old words:

" '. . . and the earth was without form and void, and darkness was upon the face of the deep . . . and the evening and the morning were the first day.' "

"Amen to that," I said soberly. That vast, rolling expanse was like the first sea at the beginning of time, the mighty mother from whose tremendous, watery womb the first life stirred toward the dry land. It was a somber, an impressive, sight.

And just then the sluggish waves broke into a glitter of flying spray, as something as long as a five-story building is high reared its small, snaky head atop its long, snaky neck out of the water.

Up and up that slender neck rose, until it didn't seem possible that any neck could grow that long. Under the sliding lucency of the sea's surface I glimpsed a fat, seal-like body, propelled through the waves by vast, flat flippers.

"Not to continue the Biblical parallels, but d'you suppose that's the serpent in Eden?" I said, flippantly. The Professor huffed and snorted.

Then he peered more closely, eyes almost popping out of his skull with curiosity.

"A genuine plesiosaurus, my boy, or I'm a monkey's uncle!" he exclaimed. "An aquatic reptile of the Jurassic, thought by some to be yet surviving in the greater oceanic depths . . . perhaps the true sea serpent of sailing lore . . . possibly even the Loch Ness Monster itself . . . gad, if only I could get a closer look at the creature—if I could but *measure* it!—I could at last resolve the old dispute concerning the inordinate lengths to which the sea monster is believed to have attained."

The old boy was hopping from one foot to another in an agony of impatient and frustrated frenzy. I had to pity him; but his torment soon dissolved into another of those moods of dreamy rapture he was constantly falling into as he regarded yet another variety of prehistoric monster.

". . . To think of it, my boy! . . . the original sea serpent of the Dawn Age, vanished from the earth before the first man stood erect . . . until now we have only been able to study the plesiosaurus from its fossilized remains—but to be the first living man to actually *look* upon the living monster itself—*gak!*"

Gak, indeed: for just then ten of the ugliest men I have ever seen came around the bluff and stopped short at the sight of us.

They were hairy and half-naked and had matted manes and beards, and hefted huge clubs and things.

And they were very definitely . . . *men*.

"Oh, my goodness," whispered the Professor faintly in a faint voice.

"You can say that again," I muttered, grabbing my gun and wishing I had packed along a good carbine and plenty of ammo, instead of one little .45.

They were nearly naked, and were about the hairiest men I had ever seen or heard of, with barrel chests and long apelike arms and thick, matted hair and dirty beards on their ugly faces. They walked with a gait somewhere between a shamble and a shuffle, huge, dirty splayed feet wide-spread, and they had poorly tanned animal hides tied about them with thongs made of gut. Grunting and snorting to each other, they looked us over suspiciously, with an expression of surly truculence.

"*Neanderthals*, or I'm a monkey's uncle," breathed the Professor, a look of angelic rapture on his face. "Eternal Euclid, that I should live to see it . . . !"

"Neanderthals? You mean cavemen?" I muttered out of the corner of my mouth, not daring to take my eyes off the pug-uglies. He nodded vaguely.

"I should have guessed at the possibility of primitive man having found his way down here, when I saw the mammoth," he said. "Both early man and mammoth must have fled here from the advancing glaciers when the Ice Age came down across Europe . . . probably via the same Gibralter landbridge the dinosaurs used, many millions of years earlier . . ."

All this was interesting enough, I suppose, but hardly relevant to the problem at hand. I didn't bother asking the Doc if Neanderthal men were dangerous, because I had a pretty fair notion they were. And I believe I failed to mention they were carrying wooden clubs, stone axes, and a couple of long, clumsy-looking spears tipped with sharply pointed bits of stone.

One perfectly enormous caveman stepped to the fore to look us over. He was a good head taller than I am, and must have tipped the scales at three hundred pounds, with those gorilla-like shoulders and huge, hairy paunch. He wore a crude necklace of seashells threaded on a string of gut around his fat throat: from this, and the way the others deferred to him, I reckoned him to be the chief.

"How," I said, lifting my right hand slowly, palm open and forward, as they do in the movies.

He grunted and spat, looking me over sourly. I took the opportunity to take a good look at him.

He must have been the ugliest man I've ever seen, with a thick underslung jaw and a heavy brow-ridge, hardly any forehead to speak of, and a nose that had been squashed flat a few times. His skin was so dirty and matted with hair that it was almost impossible to tell what color it was. His hair, amusingly, was reddish, nearly the same shade as the mammoth's coat. His eyes caught my attention: one of them was blank white, obviously blinded either from a cataract or an injury. The other eye was small and mean, buried in a pit of gristle under that bony shelf of a brow. His beard was short and scrubby, and he was crawling with lice: I know this for a fact, for while he was giving me the once-over, he plucked one of the vermin from his armpit, and cracked it between his teeth.

"Tasty, I'll bet," I remarked in an easy, conversational manner. "I can just imagine what your table manners are like!"

"Be careful, my boy, you might make him angry," muttered the Professor nervously.

I grinned. The Neanderthal man evidently felt he was being talked about, or laughed at—or, possibly, both. Grunting, he spat between my feet, a murderous gleam in his one good eye.

In the next instant he came at me in a rush, growling like a lion at the charge.

I went for the automatic at my waist, but didn't have time to use it. For the caveman slammed the flat of his stone axe up alongside my head, and, for me, the day was over.

Part Three

Part Three

MEN OF THE STONE AGE

Chapter 9.

CAPTIVES OF
THE CAVEMEN

The next two or three days I will skip over, partly because my memory of them is rather blurred, but mostly because there really wasn't much that happened to us that will bear repeating.

The Neanderthal men seem to have been on a slave-hunting expedition, and were on their way back home with a dozen other captives when they encountered the two of us. One-Eye, as I came to call the chief of the expedition, didn't mind adding a couple more captives to his collection, although I understand he thought the Professor a bit too scrawny to be worth carrying along. One of his cronies, an ugly customer I came to think of as Fatso from his triple chin and enormous belly, must have persuaded him otherwise, for when I came out of my little nap, there the two of us were, tied together.

I was being carried over the shoulder of one brawny youth who was quite glad to put me down once it was understood I was awake and could walk. These men bore little resemblance to the Neanderthals; in fact, if you shaved them and put some clothes on them, they would not look out of place on Broadway or Main Street, being tall, bronzed, athletic young fellows with straw-yellow hair and blue eyes.

"Obviously, descendants of Cro-Magnon man," the Professor explained when I got a chance to ask him about our fellow-captives. "The two major genera of Homo sapiens were contemporaneous to some extent; their respective eras overlapped a trifle."

The differences between the two were certainly distinct. The blond Cro-Magnons stood tall and straight, and walked with a lithe, limber step that was very unlike the bowlegged

65

shamble of the apelike Neanderthal men. Also, they kept themselves cleaner and wore well-tanned hides and furs. They even sported something like boots: well, high-laced buskins, anyway. And whereas the Apemen wore seashells threaded on a bit of gut, the Cro-Magnons wore polished, colored pebbles and the fangs of beasts on thin leather thongs. More than a few of them had ornaments of hammered copper or bronze, which fascinated the Professor.

"Obviously, time has not stood still for the higher orders, even here in Zanthodon," he mused thoughtfully. "They were men of Stone Age back in Europe before the glaciers came down from the north . . . but here, they have already entered the Bronze Age . . . this is fascinating, my boy! What a book I shall be able to write, once we have returned to civilization!"

I didn't bother pointing out to him that our return to civilization was probably going to be postponed for a while, due to slavery.

The Apemen—I'm going to call them that from now on, because "Neanderthal" is a bit of a jaw-breaker—led us along through the jungles at a rapid trot. They used scouts which fanned out to all sides of the slave column, which I thought was a rather sophisticated strategy for such primitives. And they seemed to know just where they were going, although how they managed to find their way home in this land of eternal and unaltering daylight puzzled me. They seemed to know where they were going, however, and from the speed at which they forced us to jog along, and the occasional, apprehensive backward glances they cast over their hulking, hairy shoulders, I got the distinct impression that they were in a hell of a hurry—as if someone were following them.

I noticed that we were following the curve of the coastline, never penetrating too deeply into the jungle to lose track of the sea, which remained at our left hand. The reason for this I did not learn until much later.

My fellow-captives were tethered to a long rope of tough, braided grasses that extended the length of the slave column, and whose ends were tied to the waists of One-Eye in front and Fatso behind. We all wore slave collars of leather and these were lashed by thongs to spaces along the length of the rope, one captive to either side. We moved along, then, in a column of twos at a rapid trot.

"My fellow captives were tethered to a long rope."

I have never worn anything more galling and irksome than that slave collar, and I never hope to.

The pace was grueling, and we were only given rest stops three times a "day" (I am going to start dividing time in this narrative between "days" and "sleeps," since it was always day down here, and "night" is hardly an apt term); during those stops, which were of brief duration, water was passed back along the line in a hollow coconut shell pierced at one end. We had a chance at such times to lie down, rest a bit, catch our breath.

The Professor and I—he was directly behind me in the column—used these opportunities to talk, while the other captives eavesdropped curiously. (I later came to understand that it was bewildering to them to hear men conversing in a language they had never before heard, since all of the human denizens of Zanthodon speak the same universal tongue.)

You may be wondering why I had not as yet fought my way free. The answer is simple: after One-Eye had nearly brained me with that stone axe of his, he and his boys went through our clothing and possessions, taking anything they fancied. One-Eye now sported my wristwatch on one hairy arm, Fatso had taken the revolver, which he wore stuck through the hides wrapped about his middle, below his enormous paunch, and another one of the Apemen had taken my hunting-knife. As for my backpack, it had vanished among the others.

Without weapons of any kind, I couldn't have put up much of a fight against a dozen savage Neanderthal men, so I concluded to hold onto my temper and bide my time. In this decision, the Professor heartily concurred.

"Rest easy, my boy; a diversion is bound to occur sooner or later, just as the mammoth appeared in time to divert the triceratops from making us his luncheon! And, besides, I am gathering valuable anthropological data . . ."

I am, of course, much to gentlemanly to have yielded to the impulse; thus, I held my tongue and didn't tell the Professor what he could do with his data.

Looking back over this part of the manuscript, I notice with some amusement that I have not yet mentioned the captive who was directly in front of me in the line of slaves.

Her name was Darya, and she was about seventeen and absolutely the most beautiful girl I have ever laid eyes upon.

Nearly naked, save for a skimpy apron-like garment of soft, elegantly-tanned furs, which extended over one shoulder but left one perfect breast bare; her slim, lithe, beautifully tanned body was as supple and graceful as a dancer's. Like all of her people, she was blond and blue-eyed: in Darya's case, the description is too sparse. She had a long, flowing mane of soft hair the color of ripe corn, and wide, dark-lashed eyes the hue of rainwashed April skies, and a full, luscious mouth the tint of wild strawberries. She was fastidious in her cleanliness and never failed to set aside a portion of her share of water to cleanse her person.

Darya was a revelation to me: imagine a girl who has never used cosmetics, never chewed gum, never gone to the hairdresser for a permanent . . . a young woman totally ignorant of deodorants, perfume, eyebrow-plucking, and the latest fashions!

For all of her primitive innocence, though, this Cro-Magnon Eve was every inch a lady—and all woman. She exposed her naked breast indifferently to the gaze of men, because her society has never found a reason to hide natural beauty away behind clothing, never having gotten around to inventing puritanical shame and prudery. When we paused during a rest stop to relieve nature, she performed her bodily functions with the rest of us, without the slightest mortification or self-consciousness.

She endured without a murmur of complaint our exhausting trek, and, although she suffered along with the rest of us from the lack of water, of sufficient rest, and of food, I never once saw her weep. Except when one of the older Cro-Magnon captives gave out and could run no more, and was callously brained by One-Eye, his corpse untied from the slave rope and carelessly tossed into the bushes. As I saw the gleam of tears in her great blue eyes, I wondered to myself if the victim had been a friend or relative.

After a couple of days of traveling across fairly level country, still within close range of the shoreline, we began to ascend a rise of low hills, and were no longer beaten until we ran at the same pace as our brutish captors. Darya seized this opportunity to attempt a conversation with me. She had spoken to me on more than one occasion, but as I could not understand a word of her speech, or she a word of mine, expressions and gestures were the most we could exchange.

I have heard it said that curiosity is the vice of women. Well, if so, I presume her curiosity must have gotten the better of her, because Darya, no longer able to endure my inability to answer or even understand her questions, promptly took the obvious course of action, and began to teach me hers.

I have always enjoyed a natural-born knack for picking up foreign tongues, which has amply served me during my travels, so it did not prove too difficult to pick up Cro-Magnon. What made it so remarkably easy was the simple fact that Darya's language was an extremely simple one, a stark matter of the verbal necessities—all nouns and verbs, with just enough adjectives to lend it tang. A language uncluttered with all the complicated tenses more sophisticated languages seem to have.

As we walked along, the cave-girl gave me lessons in the one universal tongue spoken the length and breadth of Zanthodon. She did this with a direct simplicity that I found refreshing—pointing to a bush, she enunciated the word for "bush," for example, and made me repeat it back to her until I got the pronunciation to please her. In a single day we got through the items visible in the landscape immediately around us, and progressed to the parts of the body. On the next day we moved on to verbs, and I memorized the words for "jump" and "walk" and "run" and "stand" and "sit" and "lie down" and "sleep," "eat," "drink," and so on.

Each morning when we awoke, she made me repeat back to her the words she had taught me the day before, correcting me when it was necessary. But it was seldom necessary. As a matter of fact, learning her primitive tongue came so swiftly and easily that I was impressed myself—I had always been good at picking up a smattering of things like Arabic or German or Swahili, but never *this* good.

It was almost . . . almost like *remembering* a language you once knew but had since forgotten, if that makes any sense.

Well, it made quite a lot of sense to the Professor, who, being tied to the chain gang right behind me, was near enough to overhear our language lessons. In fact, he became absolutely livid with excitement.

". . . Did you hear that, my boy?" he burbled, awe-struck. "The word for 'father' is *vator* . . . amazing!"

"What's so amazing about it?"

"Because the ancient Sanskrit word for 'father' is very, very close to it in sound: *pitar*. . . . I have been noticing how very many of the words your little lady has been teaching you are remarkably similar to the words in our own language of the Upper World . . . and I have always had a theory about the common source of all languages. . . ."

"Well, why not?" I grinned, shaking my head. "You seem to have a theory about nearly everything."

Darya listened uncomprehendingly to this exchange, her head tilted a little to one side and a quizzical expression on her sweet face.

Paying me no attention, the Professor rambled on excitedly.

"You must know, my boy, that English, French, Italian, German, Spanish and many other modern languages stem from the decay of the ancient Latin tongue . . . well, Latin, Greek, Hindi and other of the languages of antiquity derive from a common source, Sanskrit. . . . Sanskrit itself descends from Proto-Sanskrit, which came from the almost-forgotten Aryan tongue, and that language can be dated back nearly twenty thousand years, to the last of the great Ice Ages.

". . . Suppose that the original of Aryan, let us call it 'proto-Aryan,' was the language spoken before history began by our own direct ancestors, the Cro-Magnon men of 50,000 B.C. Which is about when I imagine this young lady's ancestors began drifting into Zanthodon, having fled from the endless winter of the glacial period . . . if my theory proves correct, we are learning earth's first and oldest tongue, my boy—what a sensational chapter for my book!"

"What does he say?" inquired Darya, impressed by the monologue. I shook my head.

"No matter," I grinned. "Old men talk a lot!"

She giggled at the Professor's glare of frosty reproof.

Just then, our captors came down the line with sticks and clubs, urging us to greater speed. So we wisely decided to save our breath for running.

When our language lessons had gotten to the point where

we could make each other understand what we were saying, Darya wasted no time in asking me about myself. In particular, she was fascinated by the clothing I was wearing—or what was left of it by this time, for my khaki shirt was ripped to rags and my whipcord breeches equally the worse for wear. I awkwardly tried to explain the secret of weaving cloth to the savage girl, but with minimal success.

She was also curious about my people—my "tribe" as she thought of it. I think she was fascinated by the differences between myself and all the other men she had ever known or seen.

The Neaderthal men, you understand, are brown-haired or red-headed, and the Cro-Magnons are almost always blonds. But I happen to have curly black hair. Another difference was my eyes, for they are of a shade of pale gray rare even in the Upper World (I was beginning to think of it that way, in caps, by this point).

I tried to explain to Darya that my "tribe" consisted of very many millions of men and women who control an entire continent, and live in enormous cities connected by airlines and railways and bus routes . . . well, you can see the problems I had. Darya could count to a hundred, but the concept of "a million" was beyond her; and the Stone Age tongue lacked words for "continent" and "city."

I think she thought me a colossal fibber as I tried to describe New York City and airplanes and subway trains. Her eyes were frosty and her manner became noticeably cool; after a time, she tossed her head, turned her back and ignored me for about an hour.

"Just like a woman," the Professor observed, with a chuckle, at my obvious embarrassment and distress.

Chapter 10.

WE STRIKE FOR FREEDOM

With time my familiarity with the Stone Age language of Zanthodon became such that I was able to talk to my fellow captives, and through these brief exchanges of conversation I learned much that I had not known before.

The beautiful blond girl, Darya, for example, came from a country called Thandar. At least, I assume it to be a country: it might be a city or village for all I know, since the Stone Age language does not seem to differentiate between such political divisions.

She was the only daughter of the chief of that country, whose name was Tharn. The Apemen had captured her while she had been on a hunting expedition with some of her people.

Among these was a handsome, sturdily built young Cro-Magnon hunter named Jorn whom I instantly conceived a liking for. He had been the fellow who had helped me along while I was still unconscious from the blow on the head which One-Eye had given me with his stone axe. He had a fearless glint in the eye and I rather liked the firm set of his jaw. And I could not help noticing his courtesy and solicitude toward Darya, how he helped her over rough country and tried to shelter her from the mistreatment dealt out at random by the Apemen. I got to know Jorn pretty well, because he was tethered at my left, while Darya was tied to the rope directly ahead of me in line, and to her left was a fellow called Fumio.

While I took an instant liking to Jorn, I must admit my dislike and distrust of this Fumio were equally swift and instinctive. He was a magnificent specimen of primitive manhood, it's true—taller than I by half a head, and with the most impressively muscular arms and breadth of shoulder I had yet seen. He was also remarkably handsome, in a slick,

73

oily sort of way—all in all, Fumio was a bit too "pretty" for my taste. And he had a sly glint in his eye that made me instantly distrust him. In all honesty, I have to admit my dislike for Fumio may have been shaped by bias, for Jorn asquainted me with the fact that back in Thandar, Fumio was a great chieftain, a rival of Darya's father for the chiefship of the whole country, and also a suitor for Darya's hand.

That certainly didn't make me like him any better!

Thandar lay somewhere behind us, down along the shores of the prehistoric sea which the Professor and I had been admiring when the Neanderthal men came upon us. This sea was known to the people of Zanthodon as the Sogar-Jad, or "Great Sea." There was another sea somewhere ahead of us and farther inland called the Lugar-Jad, or "Lesser Sea," which I heard mentioned when I was sufficiently familiar enough with the language to be able to understand conversations between the savages.

As for the Apemen, their country was called Kor, and it lay across the sea on a large island called Ganadol. It was toward this country of Kor that we were presently heading with all such speed as the Apemen could force out of us. I presumed their urgent desire to return to Kor stemmed from the fear that Darya's father, Tharn, and his warriors, might be on their tracks at this very moment, striving to recapture his daughter.

I had no way of guessing how the Apemen planned to cross the Sogar-Jad to their island kingdom; from their primitive weapons and accouterments, they certainly didn't seem sophisticated enough to have invented anything like boats.

During one of our brief rest stops, I fell into conversation with Jorn, the young hunter whom I liked. I asked him why the Apemen—they were called "Drugars" by the Cro-Magnons: the name meant something like "the Ugly Ones"—had come so far down the coast of the Great Sea, merely to capture a few slaves.

He gave me a solemn look. "In your country, Eric Carstairs, are not the women considered sacred?" he inquired.

"We treat them with considerable respect," I admitted. He shrugged his strong, tanned shoulders.

"Well, in Thandar we regard them as the precious vessels of the future," he said firmly. "For it is from their wombs that the warriors and chieftains and hunters of the next generation will spring into being. Without women, a tribe will soon perish."

"I can understand that way of thinking," I nodded.

"The Drugars have no women of their own, or very few," he continued. "And those that are born are very ugly—"

"Uglier even than the males?" I asked with a grin. "That is difficult to believe, Jorn!"

He flashed white teeth in a somber smile. "Nevertheless, Eric Carstairs, it is so. Even the male Drugars loathe and shun them. Therefore, they steal the women from other tribes, whenever they can find them. Always, the most beautiful women, for they hope thereby to breed stronger sons and less repulsive females . . ."

Something within me tightened at the thought of the slim, tender body of Darya crushed in the hairy embrace of a shaggy Ape-man like One-Eye. And my revulsion must have been visible in my features, for Jorn smiled, and laid his hand on my shoulder.

"Now you understand why there has always been war between the men of Thandar and the Drugars," he said quietly. "For they are stronger and more numerous than we, and for generations we have seen our wives and daughters and sisters carried off into the most horrible form of slavery by the Ugly Ones."

"Why, then, did they capture only one woman?" I inquired.

His face was somber. "The Drugars were not on a woman-hunting expedition this time, and seized the maiden Darya only by chance. Once they realized who she was, they knew that they had captured a valuable prize, and they are making tracks to return to the safety of their island country before Darya's father, Tharn of Thandar, catches up to them."

"I see . . ."

"Yes, Eric Carstairs: she is the gomad, and they mean to demand of her father many young and beautiful women in ransom for her safe return."

I already understood that the High Chief of the Cro-Magnon tribe was called the Omad, or king. Darya, then, was the gomad, or princess of her people, and would doubtless inherit the rule after her sire. If she had been a boy, she would have been the jamad or prince. This struck me as rather sophisticated for what were, after all, only a Stone Age people, so I asked Jorn about that.

"Is the chiefship of your tribe, then, a matter of inheritance rather than a prize to be won in personal combat by the strongest challenger?"

He shrugged. "Not exactly . . . if an Omad has only a daughter to succeed him, the strongest and most brave of the warriors contest for her hand, and the gomad must wed the victor. . . ."

That certainly gave me something to think about.

"Since Tharn is still the Omad of your tribe, how, then, can you call Fumio the leading suitor for her hand?" I demanded, unable to understand the implied contradictions.

Jorn smiled. "It *is* a little complicated, Eric Carstairs . . . what I meant to say was that Fumio has already declared his willingness to do battle against any challenger for the hand of Darya. And thus far, none of the warriors or chieftains of the tribe have dared accept his challenge, for he is the mightiest of us all."

I had to admit that Fumio was a tall and very powerfully built man, for all his pretty looks and sly, cunning ways. He was, in fact, the most muscular of all the men of Zanthodon I had yet encountered, except for the Apemen themselves.

"And how does Darya feel about this?" I dared to ask. Jorn spread his hands in resignation.

"Our women are not permitted to select their own mates," he told me. "Since her mate will father the children who will grow into future chieftains of the tribe, it is her duty toward the future of Thandar to accept the greatest and most powerful champion."

"But does she *like* Fumio?"

"That you shall have to inquire of Darya herself," he replied.

By the middle of the next day we reached a point along the coast from which, I was given to understand, we were to embark for the island of Ganadol.

Concealed beneath the reeds I was surprised to discover a row of crude canoes—mere hollowed-out logs they were, but doubtless seaworthy for all their crudeness.

The Apemen made haste to drive their captives into these

rude seacraft, but this required untying us from the long rope, since otherwise all of the captives would have had to ride in the same canoe, and there was not one that was capacious enough to accommodate so many.

And this looked to me like the best chance to escape that had yet come our way. I said as much to the Professor and to Jorn and Darya in a low voice. The Professor blinked at me dubiously from behind his owlish spectacles.

"And how do you plan to fight off a dozen Neanderthals, my boy?" he inquired testily.

"I don't," I replied. "The important thing is to get Darya away from the Apemen. We will stage a slave-revolt, and half of the Cro-Magnons will run in one direction while you and I, Darya and Jorn will go in the other. In the confusion, it may well prove that the Drugars will pursue the wrong bunch. Listen, it's worth a try, anyway! Once we get across the sea to Kor, there will be no chance of making an escape with half an ocean between us and safety. Now pass the word along . . ."

While the Drugars were engaged in loading aboard their weapons and provisions, the word of my plan went down the line of tethered captives in a whisper. I saw the glint of approval in the eyes of the stalwart blond savages; it was obvious that they would risk all for the chance of getting their princess to freedom.

Grunting coarse oaths in their guttural voices, the Apemen waddled down the line of their captives, untethering us one by one from the main rope to which our slave collars were attached. When they were finished and we stood, for the moment, free, I seized my brief opportunity—

Roaring a wild rebel yell, I slammed my balled fist into the hairy paunch of the Drugar who was nearest me. He gasped, gagged, clutched at his belly, and fell forward into the mud.

That blow was the signal the Cro-Magnons had been waiting for. Hurling themselves upon the ponderous and slow-thinking Neanderthals, they broke free, sprinting to freedom. The larger group of men ran up along the shore, vanishing in a tall stand of tree-ferns. I caught the Professor and Darya by the arm, propelling them forward in the other direction.

As my companions pelted along ahead of me, I dropped back, glancing over my shoulder. Most of the Apemen hovered indecisively, flapping their long arms and uttering bestial growls of rage, working themselves up into a fury. One or two of them were already heading in our direction, with Fatso waddling along in the fore. My eye dropped to the girdle of skins which circled his fat stomach.

Therein gleamed the blued-steel barrel of my .45!

As my companions entered the shelter of the trees, I permitted my pace to slow, falling back so as to allow Fatso to catch up to me. I affected a limp, dragging my left foot as though I had injured it when I broke free.

Raising his heavy club over his head and uttering thunderous growls of vindictive rage, the Apeman descended upon me—

Only to fall flat on his face when I whirled and kicked his clumsy feet out from under him!

I leaped upon him, setting my knee in the small of his back and pressing his face into the earth with one hand while, with my other, I clutched for the automatic pistol. Alas, it was pinned beneath his writhing bulk and I could not prise it free without permitting the Apeman to get to his feet again. As he probably outweighed me by ninety pounds, at least, and had worked himself into a murderous fury by this time, I did not care to face him, much preferring to kneel astride the Neanderthal.

The first of the other Apemen to catch up to me was the one I called One-Eye, the leader of the slave-raiders.

He was in a roaring fury, spittle foaming at the corners of his loose lips, bedabbling his matted beard. Forgotten was the stone axe at his waist: arms spread wide, he came thundering down upon me like a charging grizzly, murderous fury blazing in his one good eye.

I sprang from Fatso's back and faced him with balled fists. There was no chance to turn and flee, no weapon wherewith to defend myself, and the huge brute outweighed me by over a hundred pounds—

So I stepped forward and slammed one fist deep into the pit of his stomach!

Unprepared for the blow, One-Eye staggered, air whooshing from collapsing lungs. He stopped dead, as if he had run into an invisible wall.

Then he spread his arms again, attempting to seize me in a

bear hug. If ever those heavily muscled, apelike arms closed about me, I knew that One-Eye could break my back.

I slammed a hard right to his jaw which rocked him on his heels, then followed with a triphammer left that made him stagger. He seemed utterly bewildered at what was happening to him, and I suddenly realized that the fine art of fisticuffs must be completely unknown to these primitive savages.

Another of the Apemen, one called Hurok, had reached the scene by now, and he was armed with a stone-bladed spear. He remained at a respectful distance, not wishing to interrupt his chief's battle: but I noticed a gleam of something like admiration flash in his small eyes as he watched me pound the larger, heavier man to a pulp.

Finally I caught One-Eye with a terrific uppercut that toppled him, just like a woodcutter's axe fells a forest giant. He went down for the count, and stayed down. I drew an unsteady breath, flexing my bruised and aching hands.

Then Hurok stepped forward, leveling his spear at my breast, the jagged flint blade just touching the smooth skin over my heart. He had me, and there was no fighting: I lifted my empty hands in token of surrender.

By this time, Fatso had climbed heavily to his feet and was glaring at me with a maniacal light in his little pig-eyes. Foam beslavered his whiskery, dripping jaws, like those of a mad dog. Balling his huge fists, he shambled forward and struck me a terrific blow in the face. I half-managed to roll with the slap and it did me little harm besides jarring every tooth in my head. But I did not resist as he drew back for another open-handed slap.

Every moment I held the Apemen here, gave the Professor and Jorn and Darya more of a margin of time to conceal themselves in the woods. I figured that while I was a goner, at least I could sell my life to buy freedom for my friends.

As Fatso drew back to strike me again, much to my surprise Hurok interposed the shaft of his spear, forcing the other to drop his hand. Growling savagely, Fatso turned to face the other Neanderthal, who said, simply:

"Black hair is unarmed and has surrendered; do not strike him again."

At this astounding statement, Fatso stopped short, blinking incredulously. Gradually, the import of Hurok's brief statement percolated through his thick skull. His fury ebbed, replaced by slack-jawed amazement.

And as for myself, I was amazed as well. I had not thought to find even the barest rudiments of gentlemanliness among these Stone Age primitives. But such nobler sentiments were to be found, at least, within the breast of Hurok.

Fatso was a cowardly bully, and did not enjoy a fight even under the best of circumstances, so he subsided, growling, eyeing me with surly menace.

Hurok gestured with his spear.

"Assist One-Eye to the boats and revive him with water," he instructed the other. Then he prodded me in the back, and drove me to where the dugouts were beached.

Thus it was that I again became captive to the Apemen. But this time I was alone. . . .

Chapter 11.

THE JAWS OF DOOM

From the upper branches of a great Jurassic conifer, Jorn the Hunter grimly watched as the Apemen forced me into one of the dugout canoes, and pushed forth into the waters of the Sogar-Jad.

One by one the clumsy primitives cast off from the shore. Paddling with long sticks, they fought the tide, emerging into the wider seas beyond. Soon the row of hollow logs, with their bestial rowers and their lone, hapless captive, blurred and faded in the steamy fogs which floated over the face of the waters.

Jorn uttered a stern oath. The young Cro-Magnon, it seems, had conceived of an instant liking for me as had I for him. It was, he thought, fatalistically, cruelly unfair for me to have been captured again, when by my plan and daring, I had freed them all: but life in the savage jungles of Zanthodon *is* cruel and unfair; in this primitive realm beneath the earth's crust, survival does not always go to the best, but often to the luckiest.

Clambering lithely down out of his tree, the young Hunter stood motionless for a moment, savoring the air with sensitive nostrils and straining his keen ears for the slightest sign that might betoken the whereabouts of his erstwhile comrades.

Detecting nothing, he struck out for the higher ground, sensibly striving to put as much distance between the Apemen and himself as could be done. He could not be certain that all of the Drugars had taken to the dugouts; and, even if they had, it might well be a ruse. It was not beyond the dull wits of the Apemen to circle back to the shore at another point, scheming to take their former captives by surprise.

Jorn had not fled with the Professor, Darya and myself, but had taken another route, running for his life. He had briefly glimpsed another of his countrymen ducking between

81

the boles of the trees at the jungle's edge, and thought him to be Fumio, but he could not be sure.

Finding a jungle aisle, Jorn picked up his pace, breaking into a long, loping stride that he could hold for hours, if necessary, without flagging.

But it was not his intention to attempt to return to his homeland of Thandar alone and empty-handed. Not while Darya his princess was lost, accompanied only by the old man.

He intended to search every square foot of the jungle until he found them, whether alive or dead.

Darya and the Professor did not go very far into the jungle before they became hopelessly lost. They paused to rest beside a pool of calm, clear water whose source was a rocky spring. Fanning his perspiring brow with his sun helmet, the Professor sagged limply onto a fallen log while Darya began searching along the margins of the pool.

"Whatever are you looking for, my dear?" the Professor inquired, after a time. The jungle girl showed him a handful of flat, smooth stones she had selected out of the mud.

"Indeed? And of what use to us are those pebbles?" he asked.

I have already described the one-piece, abbreviated fur garment that was Darya's only attire, with its brief short skirt covering her upper thighs. Well, she reached down and pulled the fur aside, revealing a long leather thong bound snugly about her upper leg—and revealing quite a lot of naked, curvaceous leg at the same time.

The Professor flushed, and hastily averted his gaze, trying to remind himself that the innocent jungle maid had never learned the puritanical trait of shame at the exposing of her bare body. To her way of thinking, her body was young and healthy and in no wise ugly or deformed: why, then, be ashamed of it or strive to conceal it behind thick garments?

Ignoring the Professor's flush of outraged modesty, the girl untied the thong, revealing a crude sling.

"Like this," said Darya, fitting one of the smooth stones into the thickest place in the thong. Then, whirling the makeshift sling about her head, she loosed the stone with a practiced flip of her hand.

The flat stone whizzed through the air, striking the trunk of a nearby tree with much the impact of a bullet. Indeed, the flat edge of the stone remained imbedded in the hard wood until Darya pried it loose, showing it to the Professor.

He pursed his lips in a silent whistle of approval.

"David and Goliath, eh, my dear? Remarkable!" he wheezed.

The savage girl, of course, did not understand his Biblical allusion; but she sensed the approval and admiration in his voice, and smiled.

Then she sobered, looking wistfully back along the way they had come. Her perfect breasts rose and fell in a deep, disconsolate sigh. It did not take a mind-reader to ascertain the direction of her thoughts.

"You are thinking of Eric, are you not, my dear?" murmured the old man sympathetically. "Indeed, I am, too . . . I fear that we shall both miss the dear boy . . . ah, if only he had not turned back to delay the pursuit, he might be standing here with us now . . . and I, for one, would feel a lot more secure, I can assure you! Your skill with the sling is remarkable; but it will hardly serve to halt a charging dinosaur—"

"The men of my people have slain a goroth with such, ere now!" the girl informed him with flashing eyes, lifting her small, stubborn chin challengingly.

A goroth is an aurochs, and an aurochs is a prehistoric bull. The feat which Darya described was a remarkable one.

The Professor nodded. "I am quite impressed, my girl . . . but nonetheless, let us hope the larger saurians do not stray into these portions of the jungle—eh? What are you doing now—?"

His voice rose to a treble, for without a sign or word the jungle maid had reached up and slipped the strap of her brief fur garment off one rounded shoulder; the garment dropped about her waist and she shrugged out of it with a lithe twist of her flawless hips. Beneath the furs she wore nothing at all.

"Really, my dear young woman, what do you think you are doing?" the Professor gasped, blushing scarlet to the tips of his ears and hastily averting his eyes from the tempting expanse of bare girl-flesh so artlessly exposed to his gaze.

"Darya shall bathe now," said the girl, gesturing at the pool.

"Really! You might have asked me to turn my back!"

"Why?" the jungle girl asked, frankly curious, glancing

down at herself as if to see what had alarmed the old man. The women of her tribe were accustomed to wear brief fur or hide garments for the sake of comfort, rather than modesty; and, for the life of her, the girl could see nothing wrong with the nudity of her flawless young body.

The Professor uttered a strangled croak, and hurriedly turned his back upon the scene. Shrugging with a little humorous frown, as if to say that she would never understand the ways of these strangers who wore so much clothing, the girl turned and slipped into the pool. Dunking herself to the shoulders she bent down, scooped up a double handful of the wet sand from the pool bottom, and began to scrub herself clean of the dust and stain of the long overland trek, while the Professor, his back stiff and the tips of his ears glowing scarlet, resolutely kept his back turned on this idyllic and innocent scene.

But other eyes were riveted upon the scene, and they belonged to a tall man whose muscular body was stretched along a low branch which extended partway across the clearing.

The man was Fumio. He had fled with the others, but, doubling back, had striven to catch up with Eric Carstairs, the Professor, and the woman he desired. To find me separated from the other two was to Fumio an unexpected stroke of good fortune. And to find the naked girl bathing, while he was able to look on from a place of concealment, was to his thought a delightful opportunity.

Cold eyes glowing with lust, he gloated upon the sleek, wet body of the naked girl as she innocently exposed her bare breasts and thighs to his lascivious gaze. For very long had the chieftain Fumio lusted for Darya the gomad and yearned to take her for his mate. Only her father, the High Chief of the tribe, resisted his overtures: Tharn of Thandar was in the lusty prime of his manly strength, and required no mate for his daughter in order to secure the peaceful succession of the office into which his stalwart and iron strength had elevated him years before.

While he lived, Tharn could rebuff Fumio's suit, as Darya had begged him to do. The High Chief was sensible of the strength and war-skill of the tall chieftain. But he doted upon his daughter and her wish was his law; so long as Darya did not wish to mate with Fumio, Tharn did not intend to force her to do so. Time enough to settle those matters when he was grown old and long past his prime. . . .

A man as strong and handsome as Fumio becomes accustomed to having his own way. To be denied the object of his desires only fed the flames of his lust, until that object grew into an overwhelming obsession with Fumio. Many and lovely were the young women of Thandar: but for Fumio, there was only one woman, and she remained cool to his advances and well beyond his reach.

But now she was well *within* his reach; now they were alone and in a hostile wilderness, with the rest of their fellow captives scattered afar. There was no one near to see or tell if Fumio should dare take the Chief's daughter against her will . . . no one but one old man whom Fumio could break in half with his bare hands.

An unholy fire kindled in his cold gaze as Fumio, trembling with desire, caressed the nude, glistening body of the young girl with his gaze, lustfully drinking in her naked beauty.

At last he could withstand the temptation no longer. Soundless as a great cat, the savage warrior dropped from the tree branch to the ground. One powerful hand whipped out, catching the old Professor across the back of his head with a cruel, cowardly blow that toppled the older man forward into unconsciousness.

Then, wetting his lips with the tip of his tongue, Fumio sprang upon the girl as, humming a careless tune, she splashed cold water over her long, glistening bare legs. Seizing her with one strong arm about her slim waist, he dragged the shocked girl out of the water and flung her down upon her back in the long grasses.

Then he fell upon her, crushing her flat, crushing her soft mouth beneath his own in a long, ravenous kiss—

It had puzzled me, when the Apemen forced me into one of their dugout canoes and cast off hurriedly, why they made no attempt to recapture their escaping prisoners, who surely could not have gone far. The apprehensive glances they cast down the shore, however, told me all: they feared that the pursuit which had for so long followed in their tracks was now close at hand.

It also puzzled me that One-Eye made no attempt at

reprisal for the whipping I had given him. I believe now that the brutish wits of the Apemen were befuddled by the pummeling I had dealt him, and he had yet to figure out just what had felled him. Anyway, he was more afraid of the force of warriors he suspected to be at his heels, than he was interested in knocking me about. So into the canoes we went.

By the time we had reached the midpoint of our voyage and the shores of the island of Ganadol could dimly be glimpsed through the thick mists which cloaked the primeval sea, I understood the answer to the first puzzle.

I had been baffled by the reasoning of the Apemen . . . why they had been content with my capture alone, rather than pursuing the other fleeing captives. Eventually, as I saw them double back farther down along the shore, I understood their plan. The Neanderthal men might be slow and sluggish of thought, but their little brains were wily and cunning. They assumed—rightfully, as it turned out—that, once assured of their freedom, the Cro-Magnons would seek the edge of the sea of Sogar-Jad and follow it down the coast to their own kingdom of Thandar.

By beaching their dugout canoes below the point to which the escaping captives could have come, the Apemen planned to wait in ambush, hoping to recapture their captives.

It was not a bad scheme at all.

But something intervened.

Our first glimpse of "something" was a sudden turmoil in the slimy waters of the Sogar-Jad; the waves broke, seething, as a snake-like head as big as a rain barrel broke above the surface. The Apemen gobbled, pointing, eyes wide with naked fear.

"Yith! *Yith!*" they yelled in a fearful wail.

The flat-browed head rose on the end of a long and seemingly endless neck which upreared far above us, swaying snakily against the steamy skies of Zanthodon.

I couldn't blame them for squalling. For the yith of the Sogar-Jad was a monstrous plesiosaur!*

---

* Eric Carstairs appends a note to the effect that the cavemen of Zanthodon have their own names for the fearsome predators who share the Underground World with them. They call the triceratops the grymp, for example, and the wooly mammoth is known as the thantor. At the end of this book I have added a brief appendix, listing and defining all of the words in proto-Aryan which Carstairs includes in this manuscript.

"The yith bore down upon us."

As I sat there in the dugout canoe, frozen with astonishment and awe, the enormous aquatic reptile overturned two of the dugout canoes with his vast flippers. The Neanderthal men fell, squalling fearfully, into the sea. Then the beast turned to survey our craft, squinting down with hungry eyes. White foam sheeted before its breast as the plesiosaurus headed straight for us.

Our canoe wobbled unsteadily, as Fatso sprang to his feet, mad with fear.

I tensed: with my hands bound behind me, I was bound for a watery grave, without the slightest hope of survival. A vision flashed before my inward eye as the yith bore down upon us: the fine-boned, flawless face of a beautiful young girl with long, sleek hair like ripe corn and huge, luminous eyes of April blue—

Behind me, Hurok grasped my wrists. The blade of a flint knife sawed through my bonds. "Save yourself if you can, panjan," he grunted.

My hands free, I sprang lithely to my feet.

Swifter than thought, I reached out, plucked my automatic from the waist of Fatso's hide garment, clenched the barrel between my teeth, and jumped feet first into the waters of the sea!

I went down like a stone, then rose to the surface with a kick of my booted feet—

Whipping the water from my eyes, I stared up—

Into the jaws of Doom!

Chapter 12.

I FIND A FRIEND

Treading water furiously, I reached up and snatched the automatic from between my teeth. I had been so briefly immersed beneath the waves, that it seemed unlikely to me that the gunpowder could have become too wet for the gun to fire; but I was about to find out—

Pointing swiftly, I fired in the very face of the monster reptile.

It was a lucky shot, and caught the plesiosaur full in one glaring eye. That eye vanished in a splatter of snaky gore; braking with a backwards flip of his flippers, the sea monster gave voice to a piercing screech of fury and pain, and, turning, dived beneath the waves again to assuage his hurt in the cool depths.

His plunge had overturned the canoe from which I had just dived into the sea. A floundering form broke the waves, arms waving wildly. I recognized him—it was Hurok, the one Neanderthal more friendly and chivalrous than his fellows, the warrior who had cut my hands free. He sank with a gurgle and I knew at once that he was unable to swim.

I shall never quite be able to explain my next action, even to myself; but it all happened so swiftly that rational thought played little part in the decision, which I reached by sheerest instinct.

I waited until he rose floundering and roaring to the surface again. Then I swam over to him and knocked him senseless with a good hard right to the jaw!

Well, there was nothing else to do: in his mindless terror, a drowning man will get a stranglehold on a would-be rescuer and drag him down to death with him.

Then I turned the unconscious Apeman over until he was floating on his back. Catching his heavy jaw in the crook of my arm, I struck out for shore as best I could. I have always been a good swimmer, but that was the most grueling ordeal any swimmer could ever have endured. Not only was I encumbered by my breeches and boots—but the Apeman I was towing along must have tipped the scales at three hundred pounds, dead weight. Also, I could scarcely breathe, with my automatic still clenched between my teeth.

How I ever made it to the shore is something I have not quite decided, myself. Suffice it to say that, after an interminable battle with the slimy waves of that steamy sea, I found myself lying face down in wet, sticky sand, with the undertow of the sea pulling at my legs as if trying stubbornly to suck me back into the clutch of the waves again.

Not far off, Hurok lay like a dead thing.

I lurched to my knees, dragged myself and the Apeman farther on up the beach, before collapsing again.

Then, utterly exhausted, I slept.

When I awoke, I rolled over onto my back and squinted up into the sun, trying to estimate exactly how much time had elapsed while I had been unconscious. Then I remembered, ruefully, that here in Zanthodon there was no sun, and it was forever impossible to measure time. I could have slept an hour or a year, for all that I could ascertain from the heavens.

My clothes were dry, however, and so was my hair; so it would seem I had slumbered for at least two or three hours. I sat up, stiffly, and looked around me.

Hurok squatted on his hams, hairy arms propped on hairy knees, regarding me with a fathomless expression on his homely visage.

I grabbed for my gun, then drew back my fingers sheepishly. For the Neanderthal man had not moved nor flinched.

Neither did he say a word.

I looked beyond him, sniffing the air. A tantalizing aroma of cooked meat drifted on the sea wind.

A hole had been scraped in the sand of the beach. Therein a pile of driftwood had been touched afire, and the carcasses of two plucked seafowl had been spitted on sticks and were toasting over the snapping flames. I had not known there were actual birds in Zanthodon until that moment, but the pile of feathers was unmistakable.

"Why did you not attack me and slay me while I slept, Hurok?" I asked curiously. "For I have been given to understand that there is perpetual war between your kind and my own."

"Hurok does not know," he said in his slow, deep voice, and within his murky little eyes a gleam of thoughtfulness flickered. Then, after a moment, he attempted a question of his own.

"Why did you save Hurok from the death-of-water?"

I shook my head with a helpless grin. "I'm not entirely sure! I guess, because you cut my hands free just before I jumped, and gave me a chance to fight for survival . . . why did you do that, anyway?"

He shrugged, a ponderous heaving of furry shoulders, but said nothing. His long gaze was steady upon me, and there was some unreadable emotion in his dull gaze.

"How did you slay the yith?" he asked after a time. "It was like thunder from the sky. Are you sujat, Black Hair? Hurok thought you merely a panjan, but no panjan commands the thunder . . ."

I understood the meaning of panjan, which was what the Apeman called the Cro-Magnons: the word meant something like "Smooth-skin." The plural was panjani. But sujat was a word new to me, and I was eager to add it to my growing vocabulary.

Hurok shrugged helplessly when I asked him to define the word, and searched for a way to describe what the term meant.

"The great beasts are sometimes sujat," he said in his slow, dull way. "And storm and flood and fire. Sometimes when Hurok sleeps he enters the sujat country . . ."

I gathered that the word was used for all inexplicable and mysterious phenomena, especially the convulsions of nature, but also dreams, if that is what he meant by his nocturnal journeys.

In other words, the supernatural! He had asked me if I were a ghost, a devil; or, perhaps, a god.

I sat up and began removing my boots to pour the sea water out of them. I set them near the fire to dry out.

"In the first place, old fellow, I doubt if I killed the plesiosaurus. I knocked out an eye, merely wounding him. But anyway, I am certainly no god."

"How did Black Hair do it, then?" he demanded, reasonably. I showed him the automatic.

"With this: it is a weapon of my people." He looked it over gingerly, daring only to touch it with one horny forefinger.

"Your people must be mighty in war, if they go armed with weapons that smite down the great beasts with the force of thunderbolts," he grunted.

I shrugged.

He gestured. "Let Black Hair share Hurok's kill. Later, Hurok and Black Hair will speak on what to do next."

Barbecued archeopteryx tasted pretty good, I must admit: oh, sure, the outside was burnt black and the inside was dripping and raw, but hunger is the best sauce, and I had worked up a ravenous appetite, what with battling Neanderthal men and plesiosaurs.

While we silently munched our bird-steaks, I did a bit of thinking.

I was not entirely sure that I could trust the Apeman. My lucky shot at the monster reptile had impressed him mightily, and my inexplicable kindness in saving him from drowning had stirred to life within his savage breast some murky emotion akin to gratefulness, true. But how long these feelings would hold in check his natural instinct to kill or take captive a panjan was another question entirely, and one whose answer was mightily important to me. I resolved to trust Hurok only as far as I had to, and not to turn my back on him.

His feelings in regard to myself were unfathomable. He stolidly chewed down his kill, glancing at me from time to time with a somber, frowning gaze, as if trying to make up his mind about something.

And I had other things to worry about.

For instance—where were we?

The Apeman had rowed their dugouts about halfway between Kor and the mainland, before turning about to double back along the coast. In the confusion, I had not really paid any attention to which direction I was swimming.

Now . . . were we on the coast of the mainland of Zanthodon, with the Professor and Jorn the Hunter and the girl Darya perhaps only a mile or two away?

Or had I dragged us up on the shores of the island of Ganadol, and were we within earshot of the Apemen of Kor?

The answer to that question was terribly important. Summoning up my nerve, I asked Hurok his opinion. He squinted in every direction, then slowly shook his head.

"Hurok sees nothing that he has seen before," he grunted. "But there are parts of the island he does not know, and parts of the mainland he has never seen."

"What, then, should we do?" I asked. "Which way should we travel?"

He shook his head again, helplessly.

"Hurok and Black Hair shall go forward until they meet either panjan or Drugar," he suggested simply. "Then they will know where they are."

There was, after all, nothing else to do.

And so began a very unlikely friendship! Hurok was no better than the average of his kind, but from some rare gene he had inherited traits toward fairness and a certain rough justice that gave us at least a common ground whereon to meet.

He had cut my wrists free on sheerest impulse, unwilling to see a brave warrior drown without being able at least to fight the waves or cling to the overturned canoe. And I had carried him to shore, because it was not in me to watch a man who had done me even a simple kindness drown while I stood idly by.

Neither of us really understood the other—a half million years of evolution loomed between his kind and my own, and that is a formidable barrier—but survival is something we both understood. And survival is easier with teamwork.

Alone in the jungle, he or I might have fallen prey to the first hungry monster or enemy tribe we encountered. Standing together, sharing the toils and the dangers of the wilderness, we doubled our chances of coming out of this experience with a whole skin.

And that was something both of us could understand.

But neither trusted the other overmuch; both remained wary, and a trifle suspicious.

"Let us take the remnants of the zomak with us, Black Hair," suggested Hurok with a grunt, zomak being his word for the archaeopteryx. I agreed, so we packed the leftovers from our lunch by the simple expedient of rolling the scraps of archaeopteryx-steak in the broad, flat leaves of a primitive tree. These Hurok thrust within his one-piece hide garment, while I looked over my own clothing with a sour eye.

My boots were still sodden and the sea water and various earlier immersions in the mud of the swamps had cracked the leather.

My khaki shirt was a collection of rags, so I ripped it off and flung it aside. My breeches were in slightly better condition, and I thought it likely that something could be salvaged of them. Borrowing Hurok's flint knife, I cut the legs away, turning them into a pair of shorts. Not bad, I thought, looking them over; and certain to be more comfortable in this steamy climate!

My boots were hopeless, though. Various immersions in swamp mud had cracked and blistered the leather, and a long soak in sea water had finished them off: using the knife again, I cut away the sodden leather, trimming them down to merely the soles and a few long thongs; from this I manufactured a pair of strong sandals.

Then we plunged into the brush and began our trek.

Neither of us quite trusted yet in the other's friendship or trustworthiness. That would come, I supposed, with time. In the meanwhile, we kept our distance from each other, warily, keeping an eye peeled for treachery.

At least while we were awake. The time would come, as it soon did, when we would be too weary to do aught but sleep, and then we must trust each other.

In the timeless noonday of Zanthodon, the urge to rest comes upon you unpredictably. One moment you are plodding doggedly along; the next, you can hardly keep your eyes open. When this happened to Hurok and me, after some hours of striking down the coast (or was it *up* the coast?), we simply climbed the tallest of the nearer trees, tied ourselves to the trunk, straddled a branch with spread legs, and caught such sleep as we could in a position so confoundedly uncomfortable.

There was no use in worrying about whether Hurok was going to stab me in my sleep, I decided. I was so bone-weary I could keep my eyes open no longer, and if he was going to stab, he was going to stab.

He must have felt the same way, for we both fell to sleep and only awoke, some hours later, to find ourselves staring into the fanged and dripping jaws of a gigantic cat—

Part Four

APEMEN OF KOR

Chapter 13.

JUNGLE MURDER

As Fumio crushed the struggling girl under his weight and pressed hot, panting kisses on her mouth and naked breasts, the girl, recovering from the momentary paralysis of surprise, fought back like a lithe and supple tigress.

It was not for such as Darya of Thandar to yield helplessly to every twist and turn of Fate. The women of her tribe were not soft and pampered weaklings; neither were their lives devoted to the latest fashions and the pursuit of pleasure. Life in the Stone Age was a continuous and never-ending struggle for survival. In a land where gigantic monsters from Time's Dawn roamed and ruled, men were at a distinct disadvantage: only the hardiest, the bravest and the most fearless could endure the cruel privations of life in the savage jungles of Zanthodon.

And Darya was such a woman! Lacking tall sons to follow him in the hunt and the field of war, Tharn, her father, had reared the girl like a stripling warrior. He had taught her to fight, to run, to search for game, and he had instructed her in the use of every weapon known in the primitive arsenal of her culture.

The only weapon she had to hand at this moment was her own naked body. True, the height and weight and strength of the villainous Fumio dwarfed her slight form and supple strength; but it was all she had and she used it to fullest advantage. One slim knee rose to strike Fumio a sickening blow directly in the crotch—he gagged, paling and clutching at himself. And, as he did so, the girl writhed free from under his heavy body and had all but wriggled free when he clasped her about one ankle in an iron grip and brought her down upon the grass again.

Lurching to his feet and spitting vile curses, he hurled himself at the naked girl. Another woman might have yielded at that moment to the inevitable, but Darya was fashioned from stronger stuff, and determined within her brave young heart never to yield, but to fight on to the end. Lashing out with one small foot, she caught the would-be rapist full in the face!

Fumio screamed as bright pain lanced through his brain, briefly blinding him. The girl had kicked him in the face, breaking the bridge of his slim, aristocratic nose, and the agony of it unmanned Fumio. Clapping both hands to his smashed nose, which leaked bright scarlet gore down his face and beard and breast, he raved hysterical threats of what he would do to her when he caught her.

Darya sprang across the clearing, and turned to flaunt her nude young body at the furious man.

"No longer will Fumio be the handsomest of the chieftains of Thandar, and desired by all of the women!" she taunted, laughing. "Now will he be as ugly as a Drugar, and only the oldest or the least-favored of the women will allow him to touch their bodies!"

Fumio was proud of his handsome face and profile, and was not accustomed to being denied by women. That the girl should inflict injury upon so mighty a warrior was humiliation enough to such as he . . . but to be laughed at, scorned and taunted by a mere slip of a girl goaded him into a frenzy.

Without pausing to think, the warrior snatched up the slim javelin he had hastily fashioned upon first entering the jungle, and levelled it at Darya's panting breasts. Red murder filled his seething brain, and all he desired now was to slay the slim nude girl who taunted and tantalized him.

Darya paled and bit her lip, realizing her peril. There was none to observe the scene of murder, and Fumio could return to Thandar without a single suspicion. All would simply assume that she had fallen prey to one of the monstrous predators who roamed the wilderness.

The makeshift javelin was naught but a slender length of pointed sapling, lacking stone blade or barb. But, flung with all the massive strength of Fumio's heavy thews, it would suffice to transfix her breast.

And she had nowhere to flee, for her leap to freedom had brought her up short with her back against a dense thicket of prehistoric bamboo through which no aperture wide enough even for her supple form to slip through could the girl discern.

A gloating leer crawled across Fumio's once-handsome visage, now transformed into a hideous bloody mask, as he grasped the girl's predicament. He could strike her down in an instant, before she could possibly find refuge. And her only weapon, the thong and smooth sling-stones, lay in a neat pile by the margin of the pool wherein she had been bathing when he had surprised her.

It pleased the cruel and feline heart of Fumio to read the stark desperation visible in the girl's wide eyes and pale, half-parted lips, and in the rapid rise and fall of her perfect breasts. A pity to destroy such beauty, he thought to himself, before he had enjoyed it . . . but, after all, once she was slain her body would remain soft and supple for some time, and there was no reason why he could not force his manhood upon her warm and unresisting corpse—

But another eye had watched the events in the clearing for the past three seconds, and red murder flared up within the heart of that unseen watcher.

Even as Fumio, savoring the flicker of fear in the girl's widening eyes, drew back his arm to cast the javelin that would pierce the naked breasts of Darya—a lithe, bronzed, half-naked body launched itself upon him from the bushes like a charging tiger.

"—*Jorn!*" cried Darya, dizzy with excitement and relief. For she recognized the stalwart and gallant young Hunter in an instant.

And it was indeed Jorn the Hunter. His trek through the jungle had carried him within earshot of the pool in the glade, and the sharp cry Darya had voiced when Fumio had attempted to force himself upon her had come to his alert and sensitive hearing.

He had never particularly liked Fumio, for the other man's preening ways and supercilious manner were offensive to Jorn's simple and manly dignity. But to find the chieftain attempting to rape the daughter of his own High Chief was an offense which could only be erased with blood. Thus had he flung himself upon Fumio half an instant before the taller man could hurl his javelin at the helpless girl.

The impact of his leap bowled Fumio over and knocked

him sprawling. Whereupon Jorn flung himself upon the partially stunned chieftain and, settling his strong hands about the throat of the larger man, began calmly to throttle the breath out of him.

The code of justice and punishment to which the Stone Age peoples of Thandar adhered had about it a certain Biblical simplicity and directness that would have appealed, it may well be, to such as Solomon. That code may be summed up in the brief phrase: *An eye for an eye, a tooth for a tooth.* And to Jorn's way of thinking, the difference between attempted rape or attempted murder and the actual thing was, at best, minimal.

It did not take long for Fumio to recover himself, for when Jorn had tackled him and knocked him flat he had driven the breath from Fumio's lungs. Now, sucking air into his starved and laboring breast, the stronger man reached up and hurled the lightly built youth sprawling.

Leaping to his feet, he looked about for his javelin, fully intending to use it upon the young hunter before he used it on the girl who had driven him mad with desire and fury.

But Darya had sprung upon it and snatched it up while her rescuer and her adversary battled, and now Fumio was brought up short, for the point of his own weapon was leveled against his own naked breast.

He took a deep breath, licking his lips, eyes glancing wildly about to either side, looking for a means of self-defense. Alas, there was none. . . .

Jorn came lithely to his feet, and hurried to stand beside his princess, unlimbering a stone dagger he had snatched from one of the Drugars in the confusion of their sudden break for freedom. He had forgotten that he possessed the flint blade until this moment, or he would have driven it to its hilt in the breast of Fumio.

Fumio looked them over, not in the least liking what he saw. The stern and level gaze and grim-set jaw of Jorn the Hunter quite unnerved him, as did the cold flame of vengeance which burned in the narrowed eyes of the girl he had sought to violate.

Fumio was not a coward, or, at least, he had never thought of himself as one before, but his courage wilted cravenly as he read a sentence of death in the contemptuous eyes of the two young people who held him at bay. From whatever lair deep within his heart it resides in all of us, Fear came crawling up within him to suck the strength and courage from his manhood.

He licked lips suddenly gone dry.

"Surely," he faltered, "you would not murder a helpless and unarmed man . . . ?

And the instant those words escaped him, he realized how vapid and foolish they were, and loathed himself for uttering them.

Jorn smiled faintly.

"There speaks a man who, one moment before, would have murdered a helpless and unarmed woman," he said. The soul of Fumio writhed at the scathing contempt in Jorn's level tones.

Darya sighed, lowering her javelin.

"But Fumio speaks the truth, Jorn," she said dispiritedly. "I cannot kill even vermin such as Fumio in cold blood."

"*I* can, my princess!" retorted the youth without a moment's hesitation. "Lend me the weapon, and we need never be bothered by this animal again—"

For a moment Darya felt strongly tempted to yield to Jorn's suggestion, which was, after all, a just and sensible one. Only a fool or an idealist lets a deadly enemy live, to strike again; but it was not in the savage maiden to permit even such as Fumio to be murdered in cold blood. She shook her head, blond mane tousling over bare, tanned shoulders.

"I cannot do it, Jorn," she said with a sigh. Then, turning to rake Fumio with a scalding glance of utter scorn, she addressed him as follows:

"Take your life, then, yelping dog . . . but go from us and be very certain that, should either of us ever see your ugly face again, there and then shall we mete out to you the punishment which here we suspend. —*Run!*"

Fumio needed no further encouragement, but took to his heels, hating himself for it. The scornful laughter of the two young people rang mockingly in his ears as he entered the shadowy aisles of the jungle, and deep in his heart Fumio promised to wreak a dreadful vengeance against those who had humiliated and laughed at him. . . .

Some hours later, as he crouched cold and wet and miserable under a broad-leaved bush within sight of the shore, enduring the lashing of a tropical rainstorm, Fumio had cause to discover that his troubles were very far from being over.

Upon reentering the jungle, he had quickly gotten thoroughly lost, for all his skills as a hunter and tracker. This was doubtless because of the fact that Thandar was a country of rocky hills and level, grassy plains, while the coasts of the Sogar-Jad were a region of dense jungles and swamps. Fumio was not accustomed to pursuing game through such overgrown terrain, and had lost his way entirely.

He had not yet bothered to attempt to devise any sort of a weapon, for it had seemed to the chieftain preeminently important to put as much distance between himself and Darya and Jorn the Hunter as he could possibly accomplish, before they changed their minds, and decided to kill him after all. And by the time he found himself beside the misty shores of the prehistoric ocean, it was too late to begin searching for something from which to manufacture a weapon, for he found himself caught and drenched to the skin by a swiftly risen tropical storm.

Now, lost, hungry, unarmed and miserable, he crouched on his hunkers in the mud, enduring the lash of wind and rain, wishing himself dead.

The first hint Fumio had that he was no longer alone came when a splay-toed foot caught him in the small of his back and kicked him face down in the mud. He sprang to his feet and whirled to stare with amazement and sudden fear into the ugly, grinning face of One-Eye. One-Eye, whom he had thought drowned when the giant reptile overturned the dugouts of the Drugar! For Fumio had lingered just within the edges of the jungle and observed the events which had followed the revolt and flight of the captives.

Evidently, One-Eye had managed to cling to one of the overturned log canoes, gaining the safety of the mainland's shore again. For there he stood grinning, hefting in one huge, hairy hand a stone axe, looking Fumio up and down.

"Ho, Pretty-Face!" boomed the Apeman humorously. "Who kick your nose in, eh? Shes of your tribe no longer hot to mate with you, when they see your pretty-face now, ho ho!"

Fumio ground his teeth in helpless rage and despair, but made no reply to the rhetorical question. One-Eye kicked him again, this time in the side.

"Me take you back to Kor," he growled. "One slave better than no slave at all . . . go push boat down into water, or One-Eye smash you with axe and make your face even uglier."

Helpless to resist the blows Fortune had dealt him, Fumio listlessly yielded and let One-Eye drive him out into the rain. He grunted and strained, overturning the boat so that the sea-water could empty out. Then, obeying the gruff commands of his captor, he Poled the rude craft out into the storm-lashed waves and began to row dispiritedly.

To be a slave to the Apemen of Kor was perhaps the most miserable of fates which such as Fumio could conceive; but at least it was better than starving in the jungle, or being eaten alive by the great beasts.

Dwindling in the distance, the lone dugout canoe vanished in the mists, and soon the rocky coasts of the isle of Ganadol loomed up before them.

Chapter 14.

A BOLT FROM THE BLUE

It had been the sudden yielding of the branch whereon I slept that had awakened me. For the bough of the great tree wherein Hurok and I had taken refuge for the night had bent suddenly, as if beneath a massive weight.

And I awoke to find myself staring into the horrible visage of a monster such as no man of my age has ever looked upon.

It was a huge, tawny cat, with the heavy shoulders and massive barrel and long, lashing tail of a Bengal tiger. But its coppery fur bore not the black markings of that beast. Its green eyes blazed with soulless ferocity and its wrinkled muzzle writhed, lips folding back to expose a crimson maw and powerful jaws armed with terrible fangs.

The canines of the great cat were fully eleven inches long, and hooked in a terrible curve.

I knew at once what it was, for I had seen its likeness in many pictures: the saber-toothed tiger of the Oligocene, the most dread, ferocious predator that ever roamed the forests of prehistoric Europe before the Ice Age came down upon the world.

Seventeen feet long it was, from wrinkled snout to the tip of its lashing tail. And that is one hell of a lot of tiger, believe you me!

Sweat burst out in cold globules on my clammy forehead, and my heart rose to choke my throat.

Behind me, Hurok muttered in a hopeless tone:

" . . . *Vandar!* We are lost, Black Hair."

The great cat seemed puzzled to find two human morsels tied to a tree branch. It sniffed at us, and as yet the lashing from side to side of its sinewy tail was casual, a matter of balance. Where the saber-tooth had sprung from I had no notion, perhaps from the boughs of a neighboring tree. And whether or not it was hunting, or had already made its kill and was going home to sleep off the after-effects of gorging thereon I had no way of guessing.

But I could certainly hope. . . .

I dared not move, nor make a grab for my gun. And I tried to hold the great cat with my fixed and steady gaze, while slowly inching my fingers toward the butt of the .45.

It uttered a growling purr, half in warning, half in curiosity.

"Only the thunder-weapon can save us, Black Hair," muttered Hurok from behind me.

I dared not speak in reply. But my fingertips crept gradually across the stained and dirtied fabric of my makeshift khaki shorts, coming nearer and nearer to the butt of the automatic.

The entire scene, I feel certain, occupied only a few seconds of time. But I have learned the truth of what some philosophers have guessed, that time is truly subjective: for I lived an endless, aching eternity during those fleeting instants before the cat struck. And I hope I never live their like again—

Suddenly, shifting its ponderous weight upon the branch, the cat lashed out at me with one huge paw, unsheathing its terrible, hooked claws—

In the same split second I whipped out my pistol and fired full in the snarling face of the saber-tooth—

And missed!

For the claws of the vandar brushed the barrel of my automatic, knocking it from my grasp, and the slug meant for smack between those blazing emerald eyes wasted itself on empty air.

And the pistol fell, bouncing from branch to branch, vanishing as it plunged through green leaves.

Then the saber-tooth sprang—

Tharn of Thandar paused suddenly as an unfamiliar noise slammed through the silence of the jungle. His outspread arms froze his scouts, huntsmen and warriors in their tracks.

"The sound came from ahead, there, from that tree," said the warrior to his right.

Without speaking, the High Chief made a curt gesture and

"The sabertooth lashed out at me."

four warriors glided through the bushes, vanishing behind a screen of dense vegetation.

The Thandarian stood, a silent and majestic figure, his fierce blue eyes sharp and wary as those of the eagle. For many days, now, he had led the war party up along the meandering shores of the Sogar-Jad, searching for his lost daughter. The spoor of her captors had easily been spotted by his huntsmen, who had tracked the slave-raiders this far without once losing the trail.

And in the breast of Tharn the High Chief burned an unquenchable passion: to find his daughter, the gomad Darya, alive and unharmed; to slay to the last shambling brute-man the Drugar who had captured her; and to return once more with Darya to their homeland far down the seacoast.

As yet, and despite all speed they had been able to attain, Tharn and his war party had not been able to catch up with the fleeing Drugars. It was as if the heels of the Apemen bore wings. And, as yet, Tharn had no way of knowing whether his daughter still lived, or had succumbed to the cruel treatment of her brutish captors or, perchance, to the attack of some monstrous predator.

Until he saw her corpse, Tharn would believe her alive and in need of his assistance. But within his mighty heart, the Cro-Magnon monarch earnestly dreaded that moment of final discovery. For life in the savage wilderness of Zanthodon is precarious and only the most powerful of warriors may for long endure its myriad perils. And Darya was a young girl, no seasoned, hardy warrior!

That strange sound that had shattered the jungle stillness an instant before was unknown to the Omad of Thandar; never before had he heard its like. Not even the thunders that growled amidst the heavens were so startlingly loud, and Tharn frowned thoughtfully, wondering as to the source of that uncanny noise.

An instant later, the leaves parted and one of his scouts called him in low, urgent tones. He strode through the thick bushes, glancing up to see an amazing sight.

Tied to either side of a massive treetrunk, a man of the panjan and a hairy, hulking Drugar faced the assault of a mighty vandar, as the universal tongue of the Underground World names the great saber-tooth of the late Oligocene and early Pleistocene Eras. The huge cat was about to launch itself against the helpless man—

Tharn of Thandar reached out and snatched the great longbow from the hands of the nearest of his scouts. Swifter than thought itself he nocked the long shaft of an arrow with a practiced twist of his wrist, drew the bowstring taut until the feather of the shaft touched his right earlobe.

And loosed the shaft with a fluid motion—

Just as I gasped over the loss of the automatic, the saber-tooth hunched its massive shoulders, tensing its hind legs, and launched itself directly at me, like a tawny juggernaut.

It all happened too swiftly for my mind to even register the danger, much less for my heart to quail in fear.

But swifter even than the leaping saber-tooth—like a bolt from the blue!—a long arrow flew to bury itself to the feather in the skull of the giant tiger.

The arrow pierced the great cat's brain, emerging with a spurt of gore from just under the left eye.

Its leap going awry, the springing cat flew past me to graze the tree bark of the trunk with one heavy shoulder. Then it fell, limp as a mackerel, bouncing from branch to branch until it crashed to earth far below.

The arrow must have killed it instantly; it was dead in mid-leap, surely.

And I released in a *whoosh* the lungful of air I had not even been aware of holding, and felt my limbs go limp and strengthless from sheer reaction. A narrower shave than that is hard to imagine, and the cat was to haunt my dreams for quite some time to come.

We looked down, Hurok and I, as warrior after warrior emerged from the bushes to examine the dead cat, and to stare curiously up at us. They were tall, handsome men, with strong, well-built bodies and lightly tanned skins, clad only in brief loincloths of hide or fur. Clear and blue were their alert, fearless eyes and yellow-gold their unshorn manes of hair.

I knew them at once for Cro-Magnons.

Which did not, of course, mean they were *friendly* Cro-Magnons.

In this savage, prehistoric world, where to survive at all requires a constant struggle against wind and weather, beast and predator, and other men, the hand of every creature is lifted in war against all else that lives.

A stranger is probably an enemy, for he is certainly not a friend.

And a dead enemy is the only safe enemy.

Such thoughts must have passed through the mind of one of the warriors beneath us, for with cold, grim features and steady hands he lifted his bow to drive an arrow through our hearts. And I sucked in my breath again, and held it, waiting for that terrible lance of pain to extinguish my consciousness.

But the tall, majestic man at his side turned and struck aside the bow so that the arrow whizzed off to lose itself among the leaves. Then this particular man strode forward to examine us with stern but thoughtful eyes. He made an abrupt, unmistakable gesture, disdaining words.

He as good as said, "Come down."

So we came down. There was nothing else to do. With my pistol lost, we were so far outnumbered as to make any sort of resistance not only futile but suicidal.

The warriors closed about us, and led us forward to where the older man stood, arms folded upon his mighty breast.

He looked us over, eyes bright with frank and honest curiosity.

"A true man in company with a Drugar!" he exclaimed, in a deep bass voice, marveling. "Never have I seen or heard the like! Tell me, stranger, are you the Drugar's prisoner or is he yours?"

"Neither, to be precise," I said with as much boldness as I could muster. "We are friends."

" '*Friends*'?" he repeated, with a grimace of surprise. "And since when do the Ugly Ones and the Smooth-skins make friends, the one with the other?"

I shrugged. "Never, so far as I know, until I, Eric Carstairs, won the friendship of Hurok of Kor," I said bluntly. It seemed to me that I had nothing to lose, and that a bit of honest boasting and belligerence might not be out of place.

" 'Eric Carstairs,' " he repeated again, pronouncing my name with a trifle difficulty. "And what sort of a name is that?"

"It is my name," I said firmly, "and not at all unusual in my homeland."

"And what is your homeland?"

"The United States of America," I declared.

His brows wrinkled at the name.

"The Un-ited States-es . . . your land must be far away, for never have I heard of it!" he remarked.

"It is very far away, indeed," I admitted.

And, in all truth, I did not lie. For my homeland lay on the other side of the planet, and a hundred miles (at least) straight up.

He looked me over again with frank curiosity, and I took the opportunity to check him out, as well. He was a magnificent figure of a man, with a physique like a wrestler, tall and well-formed, and straight as a sword blade. A man past his first youth, obviously, but in the full and glorious prime of his life.

His features were regular, even handsome in a strong, commanding way, with eagle-sharp blue eyes, a lofty brow and a strong, good jaw framed in thick yellow hair and a thick curly beard, like a Viking chief. Heavy blond mustaches swept back to either side of his mouth, and his head was crowned with a peculiar headdress whose chief ornaments were two curved ivory fangs from the jaws of just such a giant saber-tooth as lay dead at our feet.

His magnificent torso was bare, save for ornaments, and splendidly developed. Here and there the scars of ancient wounds marred the clear, tanned flesh. A triple necklace of the fangs of beasts encircled his strong throat. Bands of worked bronze clasped him at biceps and muscular wrist. All he wore for clothing was a brief loincloth of dappled fur, but his feet were clad in high-laced buskins of tanned leather. At his waist he bore a bronze dagger sheathed in reptile skin. His mien was imperious, commanding. At once I knew him for a king.

I have met a couple of kings in my time. Once you have met one, you can recognize another at a glance. They have a look to them, something about the eyes and something in the set of the shoulders that is unmistakable.

They have the look of eagles.

And this man was the most impressive and majestic figure I have ever encountered.

He was examining me with as much interest as I was examining him. I could tell from the way his fine brow crinkled that he had never before seen a man with black, curly hair and clear gray eyes. I believe I have already mentioned that the Neanderthals all had either red or brown hair, and that the Cro-Magnons were uniformly blond and blue-eyed. If any other peoples shared the jungle world of Zanthodon with these two races, I had yet to encounter them and had no idea as to their coloration; I believed myself to be unique in this Underground World.

His keen eyes upon my curly black hair, this primeval monarch addressed me with yet another question.

"Are you from the country of Zar, perchance, or from the land of the Men-Who-Ride-Upon-Water?"

I shook my head.

"I have never heard of Zar," I said firmly, "and have no idea where it is. And I do not even know what you mean by 'the Men-Who-Ride-Upon-Water.' "

Baffled, he shrugged slightly, giving up the mystery. Then, squaring his magnificent shoulders, he said:

"I am Tharn, Omad of Thandar, a country farther down the coast," he declared in a ringing voice.

And at those glad words my heart leaped with thankfulness.

"If you are truly Tharn of Thandar," I said, a trifle unsteadily, "then I have good news for you. For your daughter, Darya the gomad, is alive and safe and somewhere in these very jungles!"

I have never seen such an expression of heart-breaking relief and joy flare in the eyes of any man as I saw then and there in the eyes of Darya's mighty sire.

Chapter 15.

THRONE OF SKULLS

One-Eye guided the dugout canoe around the rocky coasts of the island of Ganadol, finally indicating with a blow the point at which he desired his captive to beach their craft.

It was the mouth of a narrow lagoon which gave forth on a bleak and unpromising prospect of sandy, rock-strewn waste, ringed about with crumbling cliffs of sandstone whose sheer walls were cleft by numerous openings, the mouths of caves.

Obediently, Fumio rowed the canoe to the beach, then climbed ashore and dragged the canoe farther up the tawny sands with the help of One-Eye's great strength.

Two Drugar, stationed atop great flat-topped boulders above the beach, obviously as sentinels, watched silently, leaning upon long stone-bladed spears.

"Ho, One-Eye!" one of them grunted. "You depart with more than a hand of warriors, and return alone, with but one panjan for captive! Has strength deserted your arms and courage deserted your bowels?"

The other guard guffawed at this coarse jest. One-Eye's face darkened furiously. He growled and spat, measuring the other with a furious eye.

"But come within my reach, Gomak," he snarled, "and you shall learn if strength has deserted the arms of One-Eye!"

The sentinel uttered a sneering laugh, but Fumio noticed that he stayed where he was and did not accept One-Eye's invitation.

Turning to the second sentinel, One-Eye demanded of him the whereabouts of one Uruk.

The sentinel shrugged. "The Omad speaks with Xask the Wise at this time," he grunted. "It is not good to disturb chiefs at their councils," he warned.

One-Eye grinned and strutted.

"Borag may warn, but One-Eye knows not the taste of fear," he declared, boastfully. "And One-Eye returns to Kor with word that will please the ear of Uruk the High Chief, aye, and the ears of Xask as well!"

The guard shrugged, gesturing. Seizing hold of Fumio's long hair, One-Eye strode up the beach and entered the largest of the caves.

As darkness closed about the Thandarian, courage deserted his heart—what little was left therein at this point, at any rate.

Within the cave-mouth you ventured down a long stone-walled, narrow way which opened out suddenly into an immense open space, as round as a rotunda, with a domed roof which lifted far above. Therefrom, suspended like monstrous stony icicles, hung long stalactites. The domed cavern was lit by the smoky flaring of many tar-soaked torches.

Against the farther wall, which was pierced by two natural openings, both hung with hide-curtains, a jutting shelf of rock formed a natural dais. And upon this stone step stood the throne of Uruk, High Chief of the Drugars and King of Kor.

It was a throne of skulls!

Grinning death-heads, their polished ivory rondures agleam in the smoky torchlight, had been fastened together with molten lead to form a monstrous chair. They were the skulls, Fumio observed with a sinking heart, of true men such as himself: of men, women and even children, were the skulls, which boded ill for his future existence in this grim kingdom.

Atop this ghastly throne there squatted the most hideous figure Fumio had ever dreamed to exist.

Uruk was seven and a half feet tall, a veritable giant. And his corpulence was such that he weighed twice as much even as the tall and formidable Thandarian himself. His obese paunch was hairy and repulsive; his sloping shoulders and long, dangling, gorilla-like arms were thickly furred. About his thick wrists were clasped gold bangles and ivory bracelets from distant Zar, ornaments of bronze and copper thieved from Thandar, and amulets of paste and carven stone.

These did little to relieve the pall of his hideousness.

His face was a thing from the blackest pit of nightmares into which any dreaming soul has ever floundred, shrieking. The tip of an aurochs' horn had long ago ripped his face in

"It was a throne of skulls!"

half, drawing up one corner of his blubbery lips into a grimace of a frozen smile. Long tusks and broken fangs hung over his sagging lips, and his face was covered with a grisly network of scar tissue.

His eyes were cold, malignant, and soulless as are the eyes of serpents. One glance into the icy, glaring hell of those eyes and you knew, as Fumio shudderingly knew, that no recognizable human emotion lived within the hairy breast of Uruk: naught but cold greed, slimy lust, bestial fury, and the hunger to inflict pain and suffering upon everything that lived.

"Well, and has One-Eye returned alone?" demanded Uruk in a piglike, grunting voice. "With a hand of warriors he departed from Kor, loudly boasting of the many and delectable shes he would return with. Instead, but one quaking panjan do I see, and good for little that Uruk can guess. . . ."

Perspiring freely—for it is never wise to anger or distress the ogre who ruled Kor—One-Eye launched forth upon a speech of remarkable eloquence for one such as he.

The leader of the slave raid knew all too well that his expedition had been a dismal failure, and that those close to Uruk who were his jealous foes and rivals would not waste time to twist the facts to his disadvantage. So he had sought out his Omad first, hoping to present them in such a light as to earn him the least disfavor as was possible under the circumstances.

As he spoke on, alternatively whining and blustering, Fumio felt his attention drawn to the second figure upon the stone dais, as the dust of iron is drawn to a powerful magnet.

The second man was certainly no Neanderthal, and no Cro-Magnon, either, and like unto no other man that Fumio had ever seen or heard of. Instead of the bowed shoulders of the Apemen, his were slim and narrow; instead of the stalwart musculature of the Cro-Magnons, his body was lean and trim.

And unlike both he was either completely bald or for some reason his head had been shaved. His features, too, were beardless. His skin was olive in hue, and his eyes jet black—shrewd, clever, calculating, and utterly opaque. No thought that writhed through the dark recesses of his brain could you discern, even slightly, in his eyes.

His slim form was clothed oddly, in a short tunic of woven cloth, and a girdle of metal plates linked together cinched in his thin waist. Soft purple-dyed buskins clothed his high-arched feet. Bracelets of a shining, silvery-reddish metal clanked on his bony wrists, and therefrom flashed and shone strange, polished gems unknown to Fumio, which blazed like the eyes of serpents in the dark.

This was Xask, the grand vizier of Kor, and counselor and confidant to Uruk.

His clever, shrewd eyes met those of Fumio. Even in the battered, blood-stained ruin of what had been Fumio's once-handsome visage, Xask saw and recognized a kindred soul, a spirit cold, greedy, clever and calculating as it was cruel, unscrupulous and hungry for power.

And Xask smiled, a slow, thin-lipped smile.

And, somehow, Fumio felt less fearful than he had a moment before. . . .

Later that same day, two Drugar guards came and untied Fumio from the center-stake of his cell and led him blinking into the light of flaring torches.

He sweated, steeling himself for . . . he knew not what. A slow and grisly end, no doubt! For the warriors of Thandar whispered that the Drugars were cannibals; Fumio did not know whether or not this was true, but he would not have been Fumio if he had not feared the worst.

Instead of the cook-pot, they led him into a clean and spacious apartment in the complex of caves which served the ogre-king of Kor as a palace. The luxury and splendor of the room and its appointments were dazzling to Fumio, who had never envisioned such before.

Urns and vases of brilliantly colored ceramics gleamed in the soft, silken light of dangling oil lamps. Rugs of sleek fur lay underfoot; hangings of richly-colored textiles adorned the walls, where smooth plaster overlay the rough stone. Upon these walls, skilled hands with colored pigments had drawn a frieze of painted monsters and naked damsels in an idyllic garden scene. A delicious fragrance wafted from an incense burner of wrought-silver. Fumio stared about him in astonishment.

A hanging stirred over a concealed doorway, and Xask entered the room and stood smiling faintly, his clever eyes reading with ease the awe and dazzlement wherewith Fumio regarded the furnishings.

"Sit . . . be at ease," he bade the Cro-Magnon, gesturing gracefully. As Fumio sank bewilderedly onto a low couch strewn with gorgeous pillows, Xask poured purple wine into a goblet carved from rock-crystal and proffered it.

Fumio gulped down the beverage, bliss written upon his visage. Accustomed to the sour beer of Thandar, fine grape wine with honey burning at its heart delighted his palate.

The two men began to talk, with Xask skillfully drawing out the other. They had much in common, and got along well together, although neither really trusted the other as a matter of course. Xask explained, in answer to Fumio's query, that, of course, he was not of the Drugar race, but had fled into exile, driven forth by relentless foes and rivals, from his own native homeland, the Scarlet City of Zar which lay far to the inland of the continent, near the shore of the island sea of Lugar-Jad.

Fumio had heard vaguely of the Lugar-Jad, but he did not recall ever hearing of Zar. Well, he thought to himself, no great matter . . .

Using the strong, unmixed wine to oil Fumio's tongue, Xask drew him out, inquiring into the circumstances which had led to his present captivity here in Kor.

At the mention of the two oddly dressed strangers, Eric Carstairs and Professor Potter, Xask stiffened alertly. He drew from Fumio with a sequence of carefully phrased questions a lengthy and detailed description of how the two strangers had been dressed, of their strange ornaments and accouterments, and of their fantastic tale of having come from some place they called "the Upper World." He listened attentively, as Fumio told how, when first captured by One-Eye's slave-raiders, they had spoken in a language unknown to men, and how the girl Darya had had to teach them the common tongue before they could understand one word of human speech.

His eyes grew shrewd and thoughtful, as Fumio, babbling by now as the strong wine loosened the constraints of caution, told how Carstairs had driven into flight even the mighty Yith of the seas with one thunderbolt from his mystery-weapon.

When Fumio's store of information was exhausted, Xask went to the door and summoned one of his Cro-Magnon slaves, a woman called Yalla.

"The slave Fumio will join my retinue," he informed her. "See that he is given a place to sleep; he is somewhat the worse for wine at the moment, so you will need the strong back of Corun to see him safely bedded down. Where is One-Eye, do you know?"

"Yes, master, he cavorts among the slave women by express permission of Uruk," answered the slave woman. Xask nodded, masking a smile. It was apparent to him that One-Eye had succeeded in lying his way out of trouble. Later that evening, Xask found the opportunity to visit the quarters of the slave women himself, and found One-Eye dead drunk and snoring loudly, between two naked girls. From the hairy wrist of the Apeman the vizier purloined the wristwatch which One-Eye had taken from Eric Carstairs.

Alone later in his study, Xask examined the instrument. He was able to make little of it, not even to discern its purpose or use; but the craftsmanship of the watch, the delicacy of its parts, all these impressed him mightily.

Xask was from a culture immeasurably more sophisticated than the Neanderthals or Cro-Magnons. His people had enjoyed hot and cold running water and indoor plumbing and advanced iron manufacturing a thousand years before civilization arose in Europe. Their jewelry and artworks, at their height, were of an extraordinary degree of sophistication.

Xask knew good workmanship when he saw it; even the master artisans of Zar could produce nothing as delicate and precise as the wristwatch which One-Eye had ripped from the arm of Eric Carstairs.

Xask did not know whether there was an Upper World or not.

But he *did* know that he very much wanted to make the acquaintance of Eric Carstairs and Professor Potter.

From them, his clever mind could extract much knowledge. And knowledge, as the wily Xask knew very well, was power.

And Xask . . . *loved* . . . power!

It took the clever vizier little more than a day and a night to persuade Uruk to launch an attack in force upon the mainland.

The ostensible purpose of the assault was to recapture Darya, princess of Thandar. Uruk required little urging to decide to send his men to war. As Xask pointed out, with Darya in their power, they could successfully demand of Tharn of Thandar one hundred beautiful young virgins from the Stone Age tribe. And Uruk was weary of his women, and hungered for fresh, lithe young limbs and sweet young breasts to handle with his cruel paws.

But the real purpose of the invasion was to capture, if possible, both of the strangers from the Upper World.

Fumio had stammeringly described the small hand-weapon wherewith Eric Carstairs had driven the monster plesiosaurus beneath the waves. It had a voice like thunder, he maintained. And One-Eye, recovering from a monstrous hangover the next morn, had confirmed everything Fumio had told Xask about the thunder-weapon.

Even if the device was only half as powerful as the two savages claimed, it would suffice to serve the purposes of Xask.

His enemies at the court of Zar had soured the Queen's heart against him, driving him forth into the wilderness to perish. Therefrom slave raiders from Kor had dragged him into a life of captivity from which his cleverness and wit had lifted him to a high position as Uruk's crony and vizier.

But for a cultured man of civilized ways, even a high position among hulking savages is a mean and squalid life. And Xask desired revenge upon his enemies, and longed to return to Zar in might and power. And the thunder-weapon of the strangers could well be the tool he needed to lift him to his former height.

In his imagination, Xask pictured a hundred Drugar warriors, armed with copies of the thunder-weapon, hurling its lightnings against the towering walls of Zar.

And Xask smiled.

And the next morning fifty dugouts loaded with Drugar warriors, including Xask and Fumio, One-Eye and Uruk himself, launched forth upon the mist-clad waters of the Sogar-Jad, bound for the continent.

The Underground World had never known so mighty a war as Xask had conceived of in his cool and wily brain. Nor had Uruk been overly difficult to persuade into the venture.

Xask had drawn a tempting picture for his Omad . . . a delectable vision of an invincible army of Drugar, shod with thunder, their arms filled with lightning-bolts, slaughtering in their thousands the warriors of Thandar, carrying off the loot, the plunder, the cattle, and the women . . . the young and tender and frightened and very desirable women . . . even the little girls.

Uruk had slobbered, grinning lustfully.

And Fumio was pleased, as well. For his price was small, merely the gomad Darya, and as far as Xask or Uruk cared, what was one young girl among so many thousands?

Chapter 16.

WINGS OF TERROR

And now let me return to the adventures of Jorn the Hunter. No sooner had Fumio fled into the jungle, than the young warrior and Darya of Thandar turned to see if the would-be rapist's cowardly blow had slain Professor Potter, or whether the old man was merely unconscious.

Fortunately, the skinny savant had only been stunned by Fumio's blow. With cold water drawn from the little pool wherein she had bathed, the jungle girl found it not difficult to resuscitate the man from the Upper World. True, he was a bit dizzy and wobbly in the knees, but these ills were minor and would soon pass.

He did, however, have a lump the size of a hen's egg on the back of his bald pate and it throbbed painfully, giving him the very grandfather of all headaches.

"The cold water will reduce the swelling," Darya assured him. "You will soon be feeling better."

"I certainly hope so, young woman!" complained the Professor grumpily. "For I am much too old for such adventures ... who did you say it was who knocked me down?"

The girl explained what had happened, describing Fumio so that the Professor could easily recall him. The old man nodded his head, wincing as he did so.

"Yes, yes, I remember the fellow well ... superb physique, but rather *too* handsome, I should say ... and I did not care for his manner, either: he was either blustering or whining all the time, as I recall. ... Well, young fellow, it seems as if you came to our rescue in the veritable nick of time!" This last remark, of course, was made to Jorn.

The Hunter nodded grimly. "I am glad that I came in time to assist Darya," he said simply.

"Is there any sign of Eric?" the Professor inquired, feeling a little better by now. "And what of those savages? Are they pursuing us?"

Jorn explained what he had seen from his treetop perch, and how the Drugars had forced me into the dugout canoes, launching forth upon the Sogar-Jad for their homeland, Kor. The Professor was downcast.

"The poor boy! Well, what shall we do now—is there any hope of effecting his rescue, do you suppose?"

Jorn shook his head. "We have no canoes, and no other way of crossing the waters of the sea to the island of Ganadol," he said somberly. "And even if it were possible for us to do so, I do not believe the three of us could do anything to help Eric Carstairs. Rather than being able to rescue him from his captivity, we should all probably be captured ourselves."

The Professor could not refute the simple logic of that statement, although he yearned to rescue his friend. "Well, then," he sighed, massaging his aching head, "at least we can escort this young lady back to the land of her people. It is what Eric would have wished us to do. . . ."

Jorn was forced to admit, some hours later, that he was quite thoroughly lost. He confessed this to his companions shamefacedly.

But Darya was quick to sympathize with the young Hunter.

"In this dense jungle where one tree looks very much like another," smiled the girl comfortingly, "it is terribly easy to become confused about one's direction. Perhaps we should rest here, find something to eat, and seize this opportunity to sleep—for we are all quite weary after our exertions."

Her companions agreed that her suggestion was a sensible one. While Jorn began to build a fire, using, the Professor noticed, flints to set the wood ablaze, Darya decided to go hunting with the light javelin they had taken from the villainous Fumio.

"If my princess will wait until I am finished with this task, I shall be pleased to try my skill while both of you rest," the Hunter offered.

Darya shook her head determinedly.

"I feel restless, despite my weariness," she said. "Continue building your fire, Jorn, while I endeavor to make my kill. I shall not be gone long."

With that, the girl strode into the dim aisles of the jungle and was soon lost to view.

"Heh! I wonder, Jorn, if we should have permitted the young woman to go off by herself," murmured the Professor a trifle nervously. "The beasts of the jungle are immense and ferocious . . . and Fumio's spear seems to me a frail implement."

Jorn smiled.

"Like most of the women of Thandar," he said quietly, "the princess is an accomplished huntress and knows well how to avoid the larger and more dangerous predators; have no fear."

"Eh? Well, perhaps so . . . still and all, I shall breathe a lot easier once the child has returned to camp, safe and unharmed!"

"That will not be long," said Jorn confidently. "The jungle teems with game, and I'll wager even at this moment Darya has made her kill."

Nor was Jorn's confidence in Darya's skills as a huntress misplaced. For it had been child's play for the Stone Age girl to bring down an uld, a small mammal that may have been a remote ancestor of the horse, and even as Jorn made his prediction to the Professor, she was engaged in gutting her kill and trussing it with woven grass ropes; slinging the carcass over her shoulder, the girl crossed the clearing, intending to return to her companions.

Now the jungles of Zanthodon, as the cave girl knew all too well, are the hunting grounds of many fierce and mighty predators. There was the heavy-footed thantor, or wooly mammoth, and the spike-horned grymp, as the Cro-Magnons call the triceratops, and many another fearsome beast as well, the vandar and the goroth, the yith of the seas, and many more.

But none are more to be feared than the dreaded thakdol. On its motionless wings, the tireless reptile can soar aloft, riding the updrafts for hour upon hour, while searching the landscape beneath it for game. While the thakdol can fight and slay, it is a lazy brute and vastly prefers to feed on someone else's kill. Like the vultures of the Upper World, whose habits are so similar, the pterodactyl is essentially a scavenger, a carrion-eater, although it will kill when it has to.

On this particular day, a monstrous thakdol whose ribbed, membraneous, batlike wings measured thirty-five feet from claw-hooked tip to claw-hooked tip, was floating above the jungle on silent wings. It was hungry, the aerial reptile, for in two days it had found but sparse rations. And now there wafted to its keen senses the fragrant aroma of fresh-shed blood . . .

Craning its scaly neck, the thakdol peered down through the tatters of flying mist, to spy a small clearing and a Cro Magnon girl striding for the forest's edge with the carcass of an uld across her shoulders.

Uttering the almost inaudible hissing cry that was its hunting call, the huge pterodactyl folded its batlike wings and plummeted earthward, falling like a thunderbolt.

And Darya was not even aware there was a thakdol in the sky until suddenly she was buffeted by drumming wings and a scaled and heavy body slammed into her, driving her to her knees.

Ghastly claws ripped and tore, striving to dislodge the carcass of the uld from her back. But Darya had lashed the body of her kill across her shoulders with tough ropes of woven grass, and they held firm even against those terrible claws.

Losing patience, the thakdol sank its razory claws deep within the carcass of Darya's kill—spread its monstrous wings—and rose on drumming vanes into the air—

Carrying Darya with it!

The jungle girl screamed in terror as those beating wings lifted her off the earth and into the air. She had not dreamed it possible that a thakdol—even one so huge as this thakdol—was strong enough to carry off a fully grown human being, although betimes its grisly kin have been known to fly away into the sky, gripping babies or small children in its terrible claws.

And in truth the thakdol labored mightily to reach the upper air, fearing to remain on the ground where it could become the prey of beasts greater than itself. Only in the skies of Zanthodon was it safe, for therein no other predator could venture. But the young woman dangling from its claws was a more weighty burden than the small brain of the flying reptile had realized, and it swayed drunkenly in its flight, just barely skimming above the tops of the trees.

Once safely aloft, the pterodactyl made for the distant cliff where it had built its nest. And it bore the Stone Age girl with it on its voyage through the misty skies. . . .

* * *

At the sound of Darya's scream of terror, Jorn sprang to his feet, snatched up a cudgel from his heap of firewood, and hurled himself into the jungle with the frightened Professor at his heels.

The swift-footed savage veritably flew through the jungle aisles, heading unerringly in the direction from which the girl's scream had emanated.

Only moments after Darya had cried out, Jorn and the Professor burst into the clearing, and stared about them, wide-eyed with amazement. For she was nowhere to be seen!

There, to be sure, was the trampled turf and blood-splattered grasses where her javelin had brought down the small uld.

There, too, her light javelin lay fallen on the turf. Jorn snatched the light weapon from the ground, examining it.

But where was—Darya?

"She cannot have vanished into thin air—such things simply do not happen," panted the Professor, staring wildly about.

"I agree," said Jorn briefly. "But where, then, is she? Had she been chased away by one of the great beasts, a grymp or a goroth, say, the grasses and the soil would be trampled, displaying the marks of their tread. But no such marks are to be seen . . ."

They looked about them. It was, of course, even as Jorn the Hunter had said: the grasses which clothed the floor of the clearing lay smooth and undisturbed, save for the small area where the ground had been torn by the soft hooves of the little uld, as it had scrabbled in its death agony, pinned to the earth by Darya's spear.

No other marks were to be seen.

Jorn bared his strong white teeth, eyes glaring. From his deep chest there sounded a menacing growl. The caveman wore but the thin veneer of civilization; beneath that layer of social custom, he was pure savage, a primitive man, filled with superstition and primal night fears.

Suddenly the Professor seized the Hunter's upper arm, gripping it tightly.

"Shh!" he whispered fiercely, gesturing for silence. "Did you hear it? What was *that?*"

Jorn had heard it too, that far, faint, despairing cry . . . so thin and weak that it was as if it had come a great distance.

His nostrils flared and the skin crawled upon his forearms. For it had come from . . . *above.*

Suddenly, Jorn threw back his head, staring into the sky, searching in all directions the misty heavens.

And then he gasped, pointing.

The Professor cried out in astonishment as he saw the same terrible sight that had frozen Jorn in his tracks: the tiny figure of a blond girl in abbreviated fur garments, being carried through the skies by an enormous pterodactyl!

Jorn muttered under his breath, signing himself superstitiously. For the reality of Darya's plight was, in its way, even more horrible than that which he had feared.

Which, after all, is worse: to be spirited away by ghosts, or to be carried off in the claws of a flying monster?

Only for a moment did Jorn linger. Then he turned and left the clearing, trotting rapidly in the direction in which the thakdol had flown.

It was not possible for the loyal heart of Jorn of Thandar to desert his princess in her peril. He would track the dragon of the skies to its lair, and then rescue the girl, if she lived. If she no longer lived, then he would do his utmost to avenge her.

Racing through the jungles, he vanished from the sight of the Professor within a few moments.

And then it slowly dawned upon the old savant that now he was completely alone and helpless, in the midst of the most deadly and dangerous jungle upon the earth.

"Eternal Euclid! What am I doing, lingering here?" muttered the Professor to himself with a wild look in his watery eyes. Clapping one hand atop his head, to hold secure the battered old sun helmet he had so carefully clung to through all of his perilous peregrinations, the scrawny savant trotted off in the direction taken by Jorn the Hunter.

"Just a moment, young fellow!" he called quaveringly after the running figure. "Wait for me . . . bless my soul, I believe I shall accompany you and lend moral support to your noble attempt at rescue . . . !"

And, summoning all such speed as his bony legs and wobbly knees could muster, the old scientist followed the retreating figure of Jorn, joining him amid the plains which stretched wide beyond the jungle's edge.

Part Five

THARN OF THANDAR

Chapter 17.

THE MEANING OF FRIENDSHIP

The Cro-Magnons were swiftly organized into four-man hunting parties and the search for Darya commenced at once. Tharn dispatched his chieftains with a masterly air of command, retaining only a small cadre of scouts and hunters to remain behind.

As his warriors entered the jungles to launch their search for the daughter of the Omad, the primitive monarch turned his attention once more to me, scrutinizing me carefully. I could tell that he was still puzzled by my black hair and gray eyes, as had been all of the inhabitants of Zanthodon which I had heretofore encountered. But he seemed more interested in the khaki fabric wherefrom I had fashioned my crude shorts, and in the tough materials of my high-laced sandals, which I had manufactured, you will remember, from the remnants of my sodden boots.

"You puzzle me, Eric Carstairs," Darya's father admitted frankly. "Never before have I seen a man with your coloring of hair and eyes, nor a man accoutered with such strange garments, which seem made from materials heretofore unknown to me. You have come a vast distance, I perceive, from your remote homeland, where doubtless you are a great chief."

I confessed that my homeland was indeed far off, but modestly disclaimed the rank he would have assigned me.

"Tell me, then, how you encountered the gomad my daughter, and of that which passed between the two of you," he demanded.

I nodded; there was not, after all, very much to tell, for the time Darya and I had spent together had been very short. I simply related how the Professor and I had been taken prisoner by the same slave raiders that had earlier captured Jorn, Darya, Fumio and the others. I told the savage monarch that we had been assigned to a position close to each other in the slave column, and that we had talked and become good friends—all but Fumio. And I told him how we had managed to escape just before the Neanderthal men had gotten us into their dugouts, and that my last glimpse of the girl had been when she had fled with Professor Potter into the depths of the wood while I remained behind to engage the foremost of our pursuers.

Evidently, my words had contained the ring of truth, because Tharn relaxed his posture of stern vigilance, and clapped me upon the shoulder.

"It would appear that you have dealt well and honorably with the gomad of Thandar," he said with a slight smile. "And for that you have won the friendship of Tharn, Omad of Thandar! But tell me, Eric Carstairs, how is it that you come to be in the company of this Drugar? For, surely, even in your own homeland, no matter how remote, the Drugars and the panjani are eternally at war one with another . . . ?"

I shook my head; it was useless to try to explain that in my country there were remarkably few Neanderthals to be found.

"Are you his captive," he inquired," or was he yours?"

Hurok watched me stolidly, waiting for my reply. Perhaps our brief acquaintanceship had been of too little duration for him yet entirely to trust me. But, since the Cro-Magnons had appeared on the scene, the hulking Neanderthal had said nothing, his eyes dull and listless, as if he expected momentarily to be put to death.

And I suddenly remembered that war was constant and unending between these two branches of primitive man, and that death or slavery is undoubtedly the fate that would have been dealt out to any other in his place.

"Neither, O Tharn," I said firmly. "We are comrades in misfortune. More than that, we are—friends."

"*Friends?*" ejaculated the jungle monarch incredulously.

I nodded. "Yes, friends."

He shrugged, helplessly. "Eric Carstairs, the ways of your people must be greatly different from the ways of my own nation . . . for never before in all of my years have I even heard of a Drugar befriended by a panjan, or a panjan who had won the friendship of a Drugar! It is true what this man says, Drugar?" he demanded of Hurok.

The Apeman stolidly met his inquiring gaze.

"Black Hair speaks the truth," he grunted.

Tharn shook his head baffledly, and shot me a glance that was almost humorous.

"Someday, perhaps, you will explain to me how this marvel came to pass, Eric Carstairs," he said "And, no doubt, in time I will come to understand it, if not to believe it entirely . . . but if you are to remain under my protection, you must part company with the Drugar here and now, for I will not share my camp with the creature."

"Hurok will go," said the other, dully. "He will rejoin his people in Kor. There is no need for the lord of the panjani to drive forth Black Hair from his camp, merely because he is Hurok's friend."

Well, I could hardly stand there and be outdone in nobility of soul or greatness of heart by a Neanderthal savage, so I stepped forward, confronting Darya's father.

"Together, Hurok and I survived the waves of the Sogar-Jad when the dugouts were overturned by the flippers of the great yith," I said. "Together we faced the perils of the jungle, and the jaws of the mighty vandar. I will not stand idly by and abide here in safety, while Hurok my friend goes forth alone into the dangers that await all who venture within the jungle. If Hurok must depart from among the men of Thandar, then Eric Carstairs will go forth with him."

Tharn stood there, strong arms folded majestically upon his mighty breast, head bent a little in deep thought. He made no slightest indication that he had heard or understood my words, but I knew I had given him something to think about.

Then he lifted his head and looked me fully in the face, and turned to examine the huge and hairy form of Hurok at my side.

"We shall speak on this matter some later time," decided the Cro-Magnon; and, with that, turned to stride away to direct the construction of the camp.

If Professor Potter had only been there, he would doubtless have been fascinated at the way in which the Neolithic warriors built their encampment.

They paced off an area forty feet on a side, driving stakes

into the turf of the clearing at each corner. Then while half of their number began raising tents of tanned hide on center poles, the remainer erected a rude palisade about the perimeter of the camp, using sticks and logs and branches lashed together with rawhide thongs.

The barrier was crude but looked stout and effective.

While thus employed, Tharn's men ignored Hurok and me. They not only paid us no attention, but did not so much as glance in our direction. I had an uneasy feeling that the two of us were in Coventry, as far as the Cro-Magnons were concerned. It partly amused me and partly saddened me to learn that these handsome, stalwart warriors were innately racist, despising the Neanderthal men because they were different from the men of Thandar, and despising me because I had openly claimed Hurok as my friend.

I could have hoped that prejudice would prove to be a vice acquired by decadent, civilized men; instead, I am very much afraid that it is a universal human weakness. This disheartened me.

Hurok was not insensitive to what was going on. He came over to where I sat brooding a short while later, and laid his great hand upon my shoulder.

"It is not good that Black Hair should be enemies of the panjani because of Hurok," said the huge fellow quietly, and with a simple dignity that made me blush for the failings of my own kind. "Let Hurok go forth alone. Always will friendship exist between Black Hair and Hurok, and doubtless they will meet again, for the world is small . . ."

I shook my head determinedly.

"That I will not do," I swore. "If needs must, we will leave the warriors of Thandar here and search for the girl Darya on our own, since we seem unwelcome among her people. But I will not permit you to face the jungle and its dangers alone!"

Something glittered briefly in the Apeman's sunken little eye; he brushed it away with the back of his hairy hand, nodded, and strode away. And I felt a bewildering rush of emotions within my breast.

For that which my companion had brushed from his eyes had been . . . a tear.

After some hours, the hunters returned. They had found signs of Darya's presence in the jungle, they reported to her

mighty sire, but not the girl herself. And a tall, leathery old
scout with grizzled locks and beard described a small clearing
where the soil had been disturbed as if by a struggle, and displayed upon his open palm a hide thong and collection of
smooth, white stones.

"It is Darya's sling," breathed Tharn of Thandar. "And
stones such as she would have collected to rearm herself
with! Beyond these things, Komad, found you aught else?"

The old scout shook his head, reluctantly.

"How far distant is this place where you found the sling
and the stones?"

The chief scout, Komad, indicated that the clearing and
the pool lay half a mile or more in the direction of the cliffs
which lifted in the distance.

"Let us break camp here, and go thither," suggested
Komad. "If my Chief agrees, we would be wise to use the
clearing of the pool as the center of our search, which can
widen therefrom in circles until some further token of the gomad Darya is found."

Tharn nodded briefly, and the men at once began to dis-
mantle the encampment, preparing to depart. During the or-
derly confusion, the old scout came over to where I stood on
the sidelines.

"The Drugar you call your friend bade me say unto you
that he appreciates all that you would sacrifice in order to be
true to his friendship," he said to me in low tones.

I had a premonition, and my heart leaped within me,
knowing what was to come. I laid my hand on the fellow's
lean, sinewy arm.

"Where is Hurok?" I cried.

"He has gone forth alone into the jungle," said Komad the
scout, "and he begs you not to follow him. 'Let Black Hair
stay with his own kind, and Hurok will rejoin his,' were his
words. And he bade me give you this—"

The old scout put something heavy, cold and metallic into
my hand. I looked down, blinking through sudden tears.

It was the automatic which the saber-tooth had struck from
my hand!

And it was thus that Hurok, hulking, illiterate savage from
the Stone Age, taught to Eric Carstairs the true meaning of
the word "friendship."

Chapter 18.

THE PEAKS OF PERIL

It was hopeless for Jorn the Hunter and Professor Potter to expect to keep up with the pterodactyl. Even heavily burdened as the winged reptile was by Darya's weight, it could traverse the misty skies of Zanthodon far more swiftly than could the two men go the same distance on foot.

However, they persevered: for Jorn would not abandon hope of rescuing his princess until he became absolutely certain that she was dead. And, as for Professor Potter, mourning what he believed to be my own demise, he was equally determined to affect the rescue of the Stone Age girl, if only as a tribute to my memory.

"It is no more than the dear boy would have expected of me," puffed the Professor, valiantly striving to keep up with the younger man.

They had left the edge of the jungle, finding before them an immense and level plain which stretched to the foothills of the cliffs which rose, dim and purple, in the distance.

In the misty air of Zanthodon's eternal day, the two could perceive little of the plain which lay about them, save that it seemed a broad and level tract of thick grasses.

Jorn searched the plain with keen eyes, but nowhere could he discern the slightest token of human habitation. And neither did he discover any signs of dangerous predators, although a herd of wooly mammoths could be seen browsing on the long grass in the middle distance.

These the Hunter ignored, knowing well that the thantors are grass-eaters and not of carnivorous habits. He knew, as well, that they are relatively harmless unless men disturb or attack them, and he had at present no intention of doing either.

"Do you happen to know this part of the country at all,

young man?" inquired the Professor, panting slightly from his exertions. The Cro-Magnon man nodded slightly.

"Only by reputation," he admitted. "During the time when Jorn was in the captivity of the Drugars, he overheard them discussing their route. They had intended to set forth in the dugout canoes for the island of Ganadol at a point where the edges of the jungle approached very closely to the shores of the Sogar-Jad. And they hoped that Tharn of Thandar and his warriors were not so close upon their heels that they would have to venture any farther up along the coast, for—as they said—that would bring them too near to the Peaks of Peril for comfort."

The Professor shuddered suddenly, as if a chill breeze had blown upon his naked skin. *The Peaks of Peril* . . . in truth the name had an ominous and frightening ring to it!

"Why did the Neanderthal men call those cliffs by such a name?" he inquired timidly.

His companion shrugged his bronzed and brawny shoulders.

"That Jorn does not know," admitted the Hunter.

But the Professor had a feeling that before long they would find out for themselves.

Without another word, Jorn again broke into a rapid, jogging stride, trotting across the plains in the direction of the purple peaks.

There was nothing else for Professor Potter to do but follow him.

When Darya awoke from her swoon, it was a time before the Cro-Magnon girl quite remembered where she was, or realized her present danger.

At some point during her dizzy, swooping flight across the misty skies of Zanthodon, consciousness had left the girl and she hung unconscious from the hooked claws of the thakdol, which were still sunk deeply in the carcass of the uld.

Thus she had not been awake when the flying reptile reached its noisome lair and deposited therein its double burden.

She recovered her consciousness in conditions so weird and frightful that, for a long, breathless moment, the Neolithic princess believed herself either blind or dead. For all about her stretched inky blackness, a gloom so intense as almost to be palpable to the touch. And to such as Darya of Zanthodon, reared in a cavern-world of perpetual day, the darkness was a thing of utter terror—

She screamed . . . then fell into a shocked silence as the echoes of her frightened cry boomed and resounded about her. From this the girl quickly discerned that she had not, after all, been deprived of her eyesight, but was trapped in an enclosed space of some sort. And, looking up, she discerned a faint trace of day far above her head.

Above her present place of confinement, daylight gleamed at the end of a tall natural chimney of naked rock, and the brave heart of the Cro-Magnon girl fainted within her at the knowledge of her predicament . . . for never could she hope to climb that chimney to reach the exit she could see far above her.

Or could she? For, if the huge pterodactyl had been able to descend through the shaft to leave her and the dead uld in this place, why could she not climb up it again? She was, after all, slender and slim, and her agile body was less than the bulk of the winged reptile.

Something crunched underfoot. The girl glanced down to see, dimly as her eyes adjusted to the unnatural gloom, that she was in a *gigantic nest* of woven reeds, littered with filth and noisome with the fetid droppings of the winged reptile.

Reaching out her arms, the girl explored the confines of her prison. Her fingers met rough stone walls, slimy stone floor, and the jagged curve of the ceiling.

It puzzled Darya that the thakdol had merely deposited her within its nest, mysteriously refraining from devouring both the unconscious girl and the carcass of the uld whose bloodscent had attracted the huge scavenger in the first place.

Then as the nest crackled under the gliding, waddling weight of some unseen creature, and a pang of terror lanced through Darya's heart, she understood the reason for the thakdol's forebearance—and the true horror of her deadly trap!

Stirring to wakefulness, small scaly forms wriggled and flopped toward where Darya crouched, hooked claws extended and sharp beaks clacking hungrily.

The pterodactyl had left her here to be devoured—*by its hideous young!*

* * *

Hurok of the Stone Age strode through the dense undergrowth of the primeval jungle, his every sense alert and wary for the presence of danger. Well did he know, that hulking veteran of a thousand hunts, that the aisles of the jungle were the dominion of the savage vandar, the ponderous, slow-moving grymp, and of the dreaded omodon, or cave bear. But, rather to his surprise, naught moved or stirred within the jungle—or, if it did, his keen nostrils and sensitive ears could discern no token of its presence.

The Neanderthal man dismissed the evidence of his senses, although he knew that betimes the predators of the jungle slept, and that within the eternal day of Zanthodon, sleep is a matter of individual need and individual choice.

Still, he did not trust the peculiar absence of danger. It might well be that all of the monsters of the jungle had selected this particular hour of all hours to fall asleep, but such a coincidence he considered to be most unlikely.

No: there is only one creature that is the enemy of all of the beasts, and which many of them have learned to fear.

And the name of that enemy is Man.

And if men were in this portion of the jungle, in such numbers that even the giant reptiles remained prudently in hiding, Hurok grimly knew that they could only be the savages of Kor. And that meant deadly danger!

Danger not to Hurok, of course, for he was one of the warriors of Kor himself, and had naught to fear from his fellow Apemen. But the horizons of Hurok's heart had but recently widened to include others besides his own countrymen. And if a large force of warriors had landed upon the mainland from Kor, they were a potential danger to his friend Black Hair, as he named Eric Carstairs, and to his friends, the panjani warriors of Thandar.

Walking now with some care, the mighty Apemen traversed the jungle, gliding through the thick underbrush as silently as ever an Algonquin brave trod the savage wilderness of early America. No more silently than the moccasin-clad feet of the Indian stepped the huge, splayed feet of the Neanderthal.

And, ere long, he paused, freezing immobile in the shadow of a great tree. For the breeze had brought to his nostrils a familiar aroma, that of the hairy and unwashed bodies of his kind.

Cautiously parting the branches before him, Hurok peered therethrough.

Lumbering along down the aisles between the tall boles of the trees there advanced into view a great force of Korians. Hurok could not count higher than the ten digits upon his huge hands, but he knew at a glance that there were many tens-of-tens. Among them he saw and recognized Uruk the High Chief and Xask his cunning vizier, and One-Eye. A grunt of surprise escaped the thick lips of Hurok when he observed the panjan Fumio to be among the host of the war party, and that he went freely and was not bound.

For a long moment, Hurok debated within his savage and primitive heart: he had only to step forward and join his fellow Korians, to be restored to his place among his people and for his adventures with the stranger Black Hair to become only an episode in his experience, quickly over and soon forgotten . . . or he could turn about and strive to warn the panjani of their peril, thus forever making himself an outlaw and an exile, shut out from the companionship of his tribe and the communion of his kind. . . .

And there passed through the dim mentality of Hurok the Neanderthal a vision of that which was yet to come, and which only he could prevent from happening. In his rudimentary imagination, the Apeman pictured a howling horde of his fellows, falling upon the unsuspecting panjani as they toiled at the building of their camp. From concealment the Korians would charge whooping, swinging their stone axes and heavy clubs, jabbing with their flint-bladed spears. And the blood of the hated panjani would flow in rivers. *And the blood of Black Hair would be among them.* . . .

Without a word or a change of expression, Hurok whirled and plunged into the underbrush, heavy feet pounding the earth as he hurtled back the way he had come with all the speed his lumbering form could muster.

To warn the enemies of his race that his people were upon them—to commit a crime against his own kind so horrendous as to be unthinkable—and to prove to Eric Carstairs that even a hulking, apelike Neanderthal can understand kindness, mercy, justice, and the meaning of friendship.

Chapter 19.

THE STAMPEDE

With a swiftness born of utter desperation, Darya whirled and tore from her shoulders the bloody carcass of the uld she had slain back in the clearing. She raised the body above her head and hurled it in the very jaws of the infant pterodactyls as the slavering nestlings writhed and scrabbled toward her.

As the little monsters fell upon the bloody carcass, Darya seized the momentary respite her act had given her. Crouching, she sprang into the darkness; reaching up, she seized and clung to the sharp stone lip of the chimney that was her only avenue to freedom and light and the open air.

For a long, breathless moment she clung by her fingertips, her toes dangling within reach of the fanged jaws.

Then, like an acrobat, the lithe and supple girl drew her knees up, hooked one elbow within the chimney, and inched her way into the shaft, inch by slow and painful inch.

It was wider than it had seemed from below, as the Cro-Magnon girl discovered, to her immense relief. She had reasoned that it must be so, since by no other route could the adult thakdol have made its entry into the subterranean nesting place. But not until she had proven this to herself, did the girl dare hope.

The rock chimney was rough and slimy with a moist exudation from the surface of the porous rock. Wedging her knees and elbows firmly into notches, the girl climbed the shaft with agonizing slowness, ignoring the pain as the sharp outcroppings scored scarlet furrows across the tender flesh of her arms and legs.

From time to time she paused to rest and to catch her breath, for the ascent was one so difficult and hazardous as to have given pause to a veteran spelunker.

And at any moment the monstrous mother might return to share the feast with her grisly brood below.

After an interminable time, filthy from head to foot, smeared with her own blood and running with perspiration, the girl succeeded in reaching the mouth of the stone chimney.

She dragged herself out up and over the lip, and sprawled at full length upon the flat rock, bone-weary with exhaustion and trembling with the relief of the tension under which she had for so long toiled.

The brilliant day of Zanthodon was warm and comforting upon her weary limbs, and the freshness of the air as the winds of this height blew past her perch refreshed the weary jungle girl. How delicious, after the stench and the terrible gloom of the thakdol's nest, to see the light of open day and to inhale the fresh, salt breeze from the inland sea!

And then she looked about, and her heart sank within her breast beneath a weight of leaden despair.

For she lay atop a flat mesa-like shelf of rock which towered many hundreds of feet above the grassy plain.

And there was no way down.

It did not take the long legs of Jorn the Hunter very long to cross the plains to where the herd of wooly mammoths browsed. His swift and easy stride was a pace which the Cro-Magnon savage could have maintained for hours, if necessary.

But the legs of his companion were far less young, and even in his long-ago youth the elderly savant had been no athlete. And so at the midpoint of their trek, the Hunter was forced to pause while his companion caught his breath and tilled the tremor in his aching limbs.

In his secret heart, the Professor was not at all sorry that his strength had given out at his point in their journey across the plains. For he delighted in the unique opportunity to observe a herd of mammoths in their natural habitat, and at such close range.

"Fascinating!" breathed Professor Potter to himself, his vague blue eyes gleaming with interest through his spectacles which, as usual, tilted askew on the bridge of his nose. He stared at the enormous beasts, taking in the thick, shaggy wavy hair, faintly reddish, which clothed the sides and shoulders of the browsing monsters, and the way the daylight gleamed on the polished ivory of their fantastic, curling tusks

He studied the appearance of the young mammoths, their fat sides virtually bald save for a red-gold fuzz, and how their mothers tended them as they waddled about, squeaking and playing.

"What a chapter this will make for my book!" the Professor wheezed. Jorn the Hunter looked discomforted.

"I think we should be gone from here," he grunted shortly. "For the thantors can be dangerous, you know, even though they are not meat-eaters . . . if they feel their young to be in danger, they can become formidable adversaries."

"Like any other herbivores, of course," nodded the Professor. "Another moment," he added in a pleading tone. "I really wouldn't have missed this sight for the world—!"

On the edge of the herd there stood a great bull with his back to the females and the young, for all the world as if standing guard. As his tiny eyes spied the two men crouched resting in the long grasses, the sentinel flapped his enormous ears and lifted his trunk, giving voice to a warning cry.

As if by prearranged signal, the females crowded around, sheltering their young, while the other bulls echoed the sentinel's challenging cry and came shuffling through the long grasses to spy out the danger the first thantor had discovered.

"Let's get out of here—now!" urged Jorn, tugging at the Professor's arm.

The skinny savant blinked nervously and wet his lips. He yearned to linger, to observe the protective system utilized by the Ice Age monsters, but the danger of alarming the mammoths into a charge was obvious.

"I suppose you are right, young man," he said reluctantly.

"This way," said Jorn. And springing to his feet, he began running at right angles to his former path, leading the Professor away from the grazing herd, hoping thus to relieve their fears.

But it didn't quite work.

The trouble was that the bulls were sufficiently aroused by now to charge after anything that moved, and when they saw the two humans in flight away from them, they burst into a stumbling, heavy-footed pursuit.

Jorn knew the lumbering monsters could not run as fast as he, but the old man was not as fleet of foot as was Jorn, and would slow them both down. But Jorn could not desert the Professor, leaving him to be gored and trampled by the mammoths. His mind racing even as his feet flew across the plain, he strove to envision a way out of their dilemma. Long before he and the Professor could reach the shelter of the cliffs, where deep and narrow ravines would afford them shelter from the bulky thantors, the enraged bulls would be upon them. And no man that has ever lived could hope to slay a wooly mammoth with his bare hands. . . .

"We cannot hope to outdistance the brutes," wheezed the professor, at his heels. "What shall we do?"

"I do not know," answered Jorn stolidly. "Save your breath for running!"

Marooned helplessly atop the flat, mesa-like peak, Darya of Thandar came to realize the danger she was in as she looked about her, despairingly.

All about her rose pinnacles and ledges of rock, and therein she espied many thakdol nests, some dilapidated and evidently abandoned, but others containing odd-looking, leathery eggs or squalling, slithering young.

The Peaks of Peril must be, she realized with growing horror, the breeding grounds of the dreaded flying lizards. Some of their huge nests were built atop slender spears of stone; others had been wedged into the nooks and crannies which pocked the face of the crumbling cliffs. And a few were built upon the narrow ledges that wound down the sides of the peaks.

The fresh breeze raised to her nostrils the unholy stench of the thakdol's droppings, and the fetid reek of rotting meat. Here and there about the peaks flapped or soared the flying reptiles, and the girl knew that at any moment one might spy her clinging to the broad shelf of the mesa, and descend to rend and rip her tender flesh with horrible, hooked claws.

It was imperative that Darya leave her precarious perch; but where could she go? Not down into that black chimney again, to descend once more into the loathsome darkness of the thakdol's nest, for death awaited her at the bottom of that dark hole as surely as it did aloft.

Seized by a sudden notion, the girl crept to the edge of the flat rock and peered down. As she had surmised, narrow stone ledges zigzagged down the steep sheer cliff. It was similar ledges along the face of the nearer of the peaks that had given her the idea.

For such as the Stone Age girl, to think was to act.

Without a moment's hesitation, she flung herself prone and wrapped her lithe arms about a projecting boss, slid her legs over the edge of the mesa. Her probing feet found the upper slope of the ledge. Testing her weight, she decided that the ledge could bear her without collapsing, and thus began her descent down the side of the cliff.

To the pampered children of civilization such as you or I, that descent would have been an endless giddy nightmare of creeping along, inching your way down a steep shelf of rock that, at times, narrowed to mere inches. Nor did Darya find the experience exhilarating or particularly enjoyable: but the daring girl did not falter or give way to her fears. Her small, stubborn chin firmly set and resolve glinting in her blue eyes, she set her back against the cliff and inched her way along the ledge which led down the cliff by slow and tortuous stages.

The savage girl knew all too well that the slightest miscalculation, the briefest moment of imbalance, a single false step, could plunge her to a swift and horrible death against the sharp rocks far below.

But she went on, and in time the edge widened into a large shelf which extended several yards from the cliff wall. Here she paused to still the trembling of her limbs and to catch her breath in safety.

As she relaxed, staring out across the broad plain, she espied of a sudden two tiny figures fleeing from the stampeding herd of mammoths.

The bright yellow hair and bronzed, lithe figure of the taller of the tiny figures seemed to her familiar. As did the scrawny legs and wobbling sun helmet of the second.

It was her countryman, Jorn the Hunter, and Professor Potter, the friend of Eric Carstairs!

Catching her breath, she saw and realized their deadly peril, for the rampaging bulls of the herd were almost upon the two.

Even as she watched they halted suddenly, the two fleeing figures, and fell prone in the grass for some inexplicable reason.

And then her view of the two was blotted out by a mystery . . . a blaze of flame sprang out of nowhere, and a plume of thick black smoke obscured her view.

Chapter 20.

THE DWELLER
IN THE CAVE

Puffing along at the heels of his Cro-Magnon friend, Professor Percival P. Potter, Ph. D., groaned and grumbled to himself. His predicament was perilous, he knew, and this infuriated him. That a scientist of his keen perception, vast learning, and brilliant intellect should be so utterly helpless before the brute strength and tiny intellect of the enraged herd of mammoths that thundered along behind them, coming closer and closer with every ominous moment, exasperated the short-tempered savant.

"What is the use of all those degrees," he panted angrily to himself, "if one cannot outthink a herd of prehistoric pachyderms?"

It was hard to do any serious, constructive thinking while running for one's life, he noticed. So he forced his mind to analyze the present situation as coolly as he might study an academic problem, while comfortably seated behind his cluttered desk.

The solution to our dilemma is obvious, he thought to himself. *At the moment, the mammoths are angry. We must replace that anger with a stronger emotion, such as—fear! But what in the world—or beneath it—would so huge and monstrous a beast be afraid of?*

The Professor recalled the battle that he and Eric Carstairs had watched from the branches of the tree, when one such mammoth as those which now lumbered on their very heels had attacked and trampled into gory ruin a full-grown dinosaur. So huge and mighty were the great mammoths, that they feared not even the terrible dragons of the Jurassic. . . .

Was there not something that all of the beasts feared in

common? A tantalizing wisp of thought tugged at the Professor's attention. There *was* something. . . .

"—*Eureka!*" he shrilled, causing Jorn to glance back over his shoulder.

"Save your breath for running," advised the Cro-Magnon shortly. But the Professor shook his head, eyes gleaming triumphantly.

"Have you still those bits of flint wherewith you built our campfire just before the young woman was carried of by the pterodactyl?" the old man wheezed urgently.

"In the pouch at my waist," grunted Jorn the Hunter.

"These grasses which clothe the meadow are dry as tinder." panted the Professor. "One spark should set them alight. And the wind from the sea is blowing directly in our faces!"

"You mean—"

"Exactly! The one thing all beasts fear, is the thing which will drive the mammoths away in panicky flight; for fear is an emotion more powerful and compelling than mere anger."

"And all beasts fear . . . *fire!*" said Jorn with a grin of approval. "Now, why didn't I think of that?"

They halted in their flight, crouching together in the thick grasses as Jorn fumbled in the little pouch of tanned skins which hung at his waist. Again and again, he struck the small flints together, while the Professor groaned and cursed and the herd of lumbering pachyderms came thundering down upon them.

Suddenly the grasses caught, and a sheet of flame leaped roaring up between the two men and the advancing monsters. Flame and thick dense black smoke soared high, like a magical barrier erected by the potent gesture of an enchanter.

The odor of burning grasses came to the sensitive nostrils of the mammoth in the vanguard of the stampede. It was the same huge bull who had stood sentry over the grazing females and their young. And as the dreaded smell of burning grass and the terrible, licking flames shot up, the bull squealed piercingly in fear, and halted, turning, flapping his huge ears in alarm.

He headed off to the left, toward the edges of the jungle which stood below the plain.

And one by one the stampeding bulls scented fire and smoke, and turned to follow him.

Within mere moments, the entire herd of wooly mammoths

was racing away from where Jorn the Hunter and Professor Potter crouched amid the grasses—straight for the wall of foliage that marked the edge of the jungle.

A sudden sound from behind her caught Darya off guard. Surprised, the savage girl turned to peer behind her.

She had not noticed—or if she had, had paid no particular attention to the fact—but behind her the black mouth of a cave yawned in the sheer face of the cliff.

And within that cave something large and heavy dragged itself over rough stone!

The eyes of the Cro-Magnon princess could not pierce the dense gloom of the cave's inner recesses so as to ascertain the nature of that which had made the sound; but she heard the scraping of claws against naked stone and a ponderous shifting of some enormous, breathing weight within the cave.

What had aroused the unknown denizen of the cave? Had it been her shrill, involuntary cry as she saw and recognized Jorn and the Professor fleeing from the mammoths on the plains below her airy perch?

There came a sound from just within the entrance of the cave, a sound like slow, dragging footsteps—

The girl sniffed the air questioningly. Her nostrils did not detect the oily, musky reek of thakdol droppings. Instead, she sensed an odor rank and powerful, like wet fur.

It was an odor that she knew from of old, in her distant homeland . . . and an odor that she and all of her kind feared.

The girl retreated to the edge of the stone shelf, looking around her desperately for something she might employ as a weapon, for the ledge she had been following terminated only a few feet beyond the shelf whereon she now stood, and in that direction escape was impossible. Although, if the beast within the black cave were the thing she feared, no weapon she might find would serve to fend it off.

And then a vast, shaggy, manlike form came crawling out of the cave, sniffing rumbling threateningly.

It rose ponderously on short, thick legs until it towered nine feet into the air. Pricking its furry ears and glaring around with hungry eyes, it uttered a menacing growl, huge hairy arms lifting to seize and crush. The claws which armed those paws were keen and terrible, and so were the great white fangs now bared by the wrinkling black muzzle.

And Darya quailed in fear . . . to her, the dweller in the cave was the dreaded omodon, the most feared of all the mighty beasts of Thandar.

But had the Professor been on the scene, he would perchance have identified the monstrous, hulking form as that of *Ursus spelaeus,* the mammoth cave bear of the Stone Age, which died out in Europe by 10,000 B.C., but survived here in Zanthodon the Underground World.

Mightiest and most dreadful of the enemies of Cro-Magnon man, the great cave bear weighed one thousand pounds at maturity, and it could have mauled a dozen grizzlies, snapping their spines or crushing their skulls with a mere slap of its huge paws, heavy as sledgehammers.

Grunting hungrily, the shaggy monster came shuffling out upon the ledge . . . advancing toward the helpless girl, thick arms outstretched to mangle and crush.

And Darya had nowhere to escape to, for the only way off that ledge was straight down, where fang-like rocks thrust skyward to impale her slender body!

Tharn of Thandar stood amid the clearing where Fumio had attacked his daughter, Darya, only hours before. It was galling to the savage monarch to be this close to his child, and to remain ignorant of her whereabouts. Darya might only be a hundred yards away, cowering in terror before the slinking advance of some dreaded saber-tooth or monstrous reptile . . . or she might be miles away by now, carried off by slavers.

Or she might be dead.

With eagle eyes the caveman king searched the trampled turf at his feet, striving to read the events which had earlier transpired upon this very spot. Darya's footprints could be clearly seen in the mud at the edge of the pool, and the grasses were torn and disturbed as though by three pair of feet. But little more than this could the Cro-Magnon read.

The bushes parted and therethrough glided the lean, grizzled chief scout, Komad. In his hand, Komad bore a crude javelin which had been fashioned from a long stick.

"What news?" demanded the High Chief.

Komad shrugged. "Little enough, my Omad," he said. "I

have found another clearing between this place and the sea. There the grasses were disturbed as though by the pawing of a small beast, and there is blood upon the grasses. It is as fresh as the blood upon this spear, and I reckon it to be the blood of an uld."

Tharn examined the javelin and handed it to me.

"Have you ever seen it before?" he asked.

I shook my head, reluctantly. It was, of course, the javelin which Fumio had made, after I had engineered our escape from the Drugars. But as yet I had not learned of Fumio's assault on Darya, or how Jorn had taken away his spear, wherewith she had slain the uld before being carried off.

"The weapon is hastily made from a dry, fallen branch," observed Tharn. "Certainly not of Thandarian worksmanship, nor of the Drugars, either."

"When we escaped from the Drugars," I pointed out, "we were all unarmed. Upon entering the jungle, any one of your people might have paused in his or her flight long enough to trim such a stick, making a crude weapon such as this."

"That is true," nodded Tharn.

Then, turning to the old scout, he was about to command him to return to his search-party, when the underbrush parted and a huge form shouldered through.

"*Hurok!*" I cried with relief. For it was indeed the Korian, my Neanderthal comrade who had fled alone into the jungle rather than impose his undesired presence upon the Cro-Magnons.

"What do you want here, Drugar?" demanded Tharn sternly, with one hand upon his flint knife.

"Hurok has returned where he is not wanted," said the Neanderthal man in his deep, slow voice, "to warn the friends of Black Hair that Uruk, Omad of Kor, and a mighty host of warriors have entered this part of the jungle and are advancing upon this very spot."

The Cro-Magnons flinched and gasped, for the news burst upon them like an unsuspected thunderbolt.

Tharn grunted angrily, eyes glaring like those of a lion at bay. "Just when we were on the track of my daughter," he growled, "we must face the Drugars in war! Well, so be it— Komad, summon my warriors."

The scout nodded, and lifting to his lips the hollow horn of an aurochs he sounded a deep, groaning call. At once warriors and huntsmen began returning to the glade of the pool, assembling to hear the commands of their Omad.

"We cannot bear the brunt of attack here," decided Tharn swiftly, "for they could hide behind every bole while we remain exposed to their missiles. Komad, where is a more advantageous place for such a battle as advances upon us?"

The old scout thought a moment, then pointed. "In that direction, the jungle ends, opening upon a level plain, with cliffs and mountains beyond," he answered.

"Then let us depart for the plain at once," commanded Tharn.

Part Six

WAR IN THE STONE AGE

Chapter 21.

THE PASS
THROUGH THE PEAKS

As the panic-stricken herd receded toward the jungle, Jorn and Professor Potter surveyed their handiwork with a certain degree of complacency and self-congratulation. And the Neolithic chieftain turned to view the old man with a new light of respect.

"It was clever of you to think of fire," said the youth admiringly. "When all that Jorn could think of was to run away ... you must be a very wise man."

The Professor preened himself a trifle, basking in the admiring gaze of the young savage.

"Ahem!" he coughed. "Kind of you, my boy, but actually no more than I deserve ... for in my own country, I will have you know, I am a highly-respected scholar and authority upon many recondite subjects. A trained, scientific mind, you know, *should* be able to cope with the small problems of the Stone Age ..."

Like most of the words which the Professor used, Jorn could make nothing of *scholar, authority*, and so on. But he gathered the general drift of the Professor's modest little speech, and smiled slightly.

"I suggest that we continue our journey, now that I am rested," murmured the Professor, peering off toward the cliffs, which now were quite near.

Jorn nodded, turning to survey the Peaks of Peril. And all at once the Stone Age boy froze as cold fear clawed at his vitals.

"What is it that disturbs you, young man?" inquired the Professor, noting his companion's sudden anxiety. "Has the wind changed, perchance, driving the wall of fire back upon us?"

153

"No," growled Jorn the Hunter, pointing. *"Look—!"*

The Professor craned his head, peering in the direction of Jorn's extended arm. And suddenly he gasped, and went pale.

For there, crouching at the edge of a shelf of stone, they both could clearly observe the form of Darya of Thandar!

She was dirtied and dishevelled by her experiences in the thakdol's nest, and the blood of the uld's carcass had stained her back and shoulders, but at a glance both men could see that she still lived and did not seem to have sustained any injury of a serious nature.

And then there loomed up above her the immense and shaggy shape of that which had caught her terrified, fascinated attention—

"Omodon!" groaned Jorn in stifled tones.

"Cave bear, for the Love of Linnaeus!" cried the Professor, almost in the same moment.

They watched, frozen with horror, as the lumbering monster advanced upon the cowering girl, huge arms lifted to maul and crush and slay. . . .

It did not take the horde of Apemen from Kor very long to find the clearing from which Tharn and his warriors had retreated, nor were the signs of their passage unreadable to the alert senses of the Neanderthal men. If their eyes were rather weak and dim of vision, as I had by now good cause to believe, their sense of smell was remarkably keen— keener by far than the sensitivity of the nostrils of civilized men, for they were closer to the primal beasts than are we.

It was One-Eye who detected the direction in which the Cro-Magnons had fled.

Crouched on all fours, the Neanderthal man sniffed the footprints in the turf. A bestial growl escaped his snarling lips as he scented a detested odor.

"Panjani!" he grunted to his Chief. "Tens-of-tens . . . they went that way," he added, pointing. Uruk surveyed the end of the clearing, his suspicious little eyes reading the passage of many men in broken twigs and disturbed fallen leaves.

"Come!" he grunted, gesturing with his axe. And without another word, the Apeman turned and lumbered in the direction in which Tharn of Thandar had marched his warriors. At his heels shambled two score of the mightiest warriors of Kor, armed to the very teeth.

Xask and Fumio, however, took up the rear. The sly vizier preferred to put as much distance between himself and any armed conflict as could with prudence be effected, and Fumio, although no coward, wisely clung by the side of his only friend among the Drugars.

"It would appear that the fears of One-Eye were correct, and that the father of the girl from Thandar has indeed pursued her captors, and in force!" observed the slender man in the silken tunic. "Now, by Minos, we shall see a battle!—but from a careful distance, eh, Fumio?"

"As you say, lord," muttered the other. Inwardly, a pang of despair lanced through his heart; for if Tharn of Thandar were indeed as near as the Apemen believed, then he stood in a position of peril more deadly than if he had rashly placed himself in the very forefront of the Korian charge.

Once Darya's father had learned of his attempted rape of the Princess of Thandar, he would be hounded into exile and outlawry for the remainder of his life, with no possible hope of mercy or a royal pardon. If, indeed, the Cro-Magnon monarch permitted him to escape with his life!

"Let us, then, follow our brutish heroes," smiled the slim, dark man, "and observe their battle against the rival host."

The two conspirators entered the jungle and followed the loping, grunting Neanderthals to the edge.

Reaching the broad and level plains before the first of the Apemen of Kor, Tharn and his host of warriors took up their position upon the sandy crest of a rounded knoll some distance from the edge of the trees.

It was not high, this shallow hill, to afford the Cro-Magnons any particular advantage, but still and all their savage adversaries would have to come at them up the slope, which would force the bowlegged primitives to slow the speed of their charge, however slightly.

Here Tharn disposed his warriors swiftly in a double ring about the hill-crest, and the formation he selected inescapably reminded me of the famous "British square." Which gave me something of an idea.

"If a stranger may offer a suggestion," I said, turning to Tharn. He grunted his assent, not taking his eyes from the edges of the trees.

"If you will arm the first rank of your warriors with bows,

and have them kneel," I suggested, "while the second rank
arm themselves with spears, and stand, one rank can dis-
charge their weapons and rearm, while the second rank fire
as the first are rearming. In this manner, you can maintain a
continuous rate of fire upon the Drugars, and bring them to a
standstill. It is worth a try, at least."

Something gleamed in Tharn's eyes and was gone.

"Your plan is not without virtue," said Tharn, frowning
thoughtfully. "Is it thus that the warriors of your people defend themselves against their foemen?"

"That is so," I nodded. While my people are American,
their ancestors were British, so it was not exactly an untruth.

In low, clear tones the Omad of Thandar passed his in-
structions to his warriors. It is to the credit of the men of
Thandar that they instantly grasped the tactical advantage of
the trick I had suggested. And I remembered reading, somewhere, that the human brain of modern man is in every respect identical with that of our Cro-Magnon ancestors tens of
thousands of years before.

Ignorant and superstitious savages these Stone Age men
might be, but their intellects were as swift and keen as my
own.

"They are here," said one of the bowmen, pointing.

We looked; hulking, hairy figures lurked within the
shadows of the trees. Daylight gleamed on the polished stone
of axe-blade and spear-point.

"Well, then, let them come," said Tharn in a level voice,
"and we shall see what we shall see."

He turned toward his warriors.

"Warriors of Thandar," he said in clear and ringing tones,
"we have come into this region to rescue the gomad, my
daughter, from her brutish and cowardly captors. Those who
attack from ambush and steal our women are before you!
They are no less mortal than are you, and their flesh may be
pierced with sharpened stone as easily as can your own. But
they are not true men, and are hence your inferiors, closer to
the bestial than are you: prove, therefore, once and for all
time, which is the superior—the Apemen of Kor, or the true
men of Thandar!"

Even as the Omad ceased speaking, a chorus of grunting
cries reached our ears, and hulking figures burst from the un-

derbrush, waddling on thick, hairy, bowed legs toward our lines.

And the battle began!

Jorn and the Professor stared skyward at Darya, who suddenly vanished from their view. The enormous form of the mighty omodon also turned from view, leaving the two watchers in ignorance of the fate of the Cro-Magnon girl.

"Do you see a way up the cliff?" inquired Professor Potter, anxiously.

Jorn the Hunter searched the cliff face with keen eyes, and shook his head reluctantly.

"The ledge which Darya seems to have been following ends shortly past the shelf on which she was attacked by the omodon," he said in grimly solemn tones.

"What, then, shall we do?" inquired the Professor, reluctant to give up, although it seemed a hopeless quest.

"There!"

The sharp eyes of the Hunter had spied a crevice in the clifflike wall of stone. It was a ravine, narrow as a man, which seemed to penetrate the mountain to some depth.

"Is it a pass through the mountains to the other side, do you think, or an entrance into the mountain itself?" inquired the Professor. "Do you think the mountain is hollow?"

Jorn shook his head, blond mane tousling.

"One cave does not a hollow mountain make," he said. "Still and all, we shall not know the truth of it until we trace the ravine to its end. Come—"

And the Cro-Magnon youth turned on his heel and vanished into the dark and narrow crevice, leaving the Professor to follow as best he could.

Chapter 22.

THE THUNDER-WEAPON

As the mighty cave bear came down upon her, Darya hurled a handful of pebbles to her right. They clattered noisily against the stone shelf of the ledge.

Its small eyes half-blinded by the sudden emergence from the darkness of the cave into the eternal day of Zanthodon, the huge beast swung clumsily in the direction from which that clattering sound had come, massive paws reaching.

In that split-second, as the beast turned its side to her, Darya acted!

Since there was nowhere to go but back the way she had come or into the black mouth of the cave bear's lair, she chose the second route.

In a moment the darkness of the cave swallowed her. The ragged stone roof was low, forcing the lithe girl to bend almost double as she penetrated the interior of the cave. The stench of the bear's droppings was overpowering, but Darya gulped air and forced herself to go on. This cave might well prove to be a dead end, but the girl would never know until she discovered the fact for herself.

Beyond the lair of the omodon, she found a very small passage which only one as slim and limber as herself could possibly negotiate. But once through it, the cavern opened to such a height that she could walk erect, although the darkness was utter and absolute.

Extending her arms so that she could feel for any obstruction before her, the Cro-Magnon girl explored the length of the cave. At its end, she found a side-tunnel which sloped sharply downward. Since she had nothing at all to lose by being venturesome, she began to trace the steeply sloping path.

It had been many hours since the girl had drunk or eaten or enjoyed a normal and restful slumber, and she was trem-

158

bling with exertion and fatigue, and ferociously hungry. But the women of the Stone Age learn quite early on to endure such privations as they must, and Darya bravely closed her mind to the ache in her weary muscles, the thirst which dried her throat, and the hunger which gnawed at her belly.

From the moment she had slain the uld everything had gone wrong, she thought to herself as she went down the steep incline in utter gloom. If only she had remained in the clearing with Jorn and the old man!

If only someone brave and strong and resourceful were here with her, to share the danger and to comfort her in the darkness . . . if only the handsome stranger, Eric Carstairs, were here. . . .

Resolutly, the Cro-Magnon princess wrenched her thoughts from such matters, and applied herself to the problems at hand.

Caverns such as this were not entirely unknown to her experience. In her distant homeland, caves were found in the sides of the hills and mountains, and the Stone Age princess knew that at times they were the homes of fearsome creatures, like the xunth, the giant serpents which infest the interior of the earth, or the vathrib, the dreadful albino spiders of the abyss.

Darya had no reason to suspect that such terrible creatures dwelt here in the mountains beyond the jungle country. On the other hand, she had no cause to think that they did not. Whichever the truth of the matter be, there was nothing else for her to do but to continue that terrible journey through the utter darkness of the mountain's interior.

To go back, to retrace her steps until she reentered the lair of the omodon, was sure and certain death.

But to continue on forward offered her, at very least, a chance of survival.

So she went forward . . . into the unknown.

The howling mob of Neanderthal warriors burst from the edges of the jungle and charged, swinging the stone axes and jabbing their crude spears, upon the massed ranks of the Cro-Magnons.

Twangg! went the Cro-Magnon bows, and the hulking Apemen went down squalling, plucking feebly at the vibrant, feathered shafts which protruded from their breasts.

Again they charged, yowling, and this time the spearmen who stood above and behind the kneeling archers bent their powerful shoulders and arms, loosening upon the shambling horde their long, flint-bladed javelins.

And again the Apemen fell, coughing blood, some pinned to the turf by the force with which the spears had been thrown.

As the survivors fled back into the jungle, Uruk, from a safe place behind the bole of a mighty tree, growled menacingly. He had not before faced the warriors of Thandar in open battle, preferring the less dangerous tactics of ambush and sudden raid. And now he had an inkling of why Xask had heretofore persuaded him to avoid an open conflict, which had hitherto agreed with his own inclinations.

"Circle around them, Uruk, and strike from several sides at the same times," suggested his vizier from a similar place of safety and concealment. "Remember, they have only a limited number of spears and arrows. Once expended, their supplies of weaponry cannot easily be replaced. At that time, it will be man against man, axe against axe, strength against brute strength. And in any such contest, the warriors of Kor are bound to triumph, for they are stronger and heavier than are the men of Thandar!"

This made good sense to the dull-witted Uruk, so the High Chief passed his grunting commands along and soon the battle began again upon that level plain under the eternal day.

"We cannot maintain this rate of expenditure," said Tharn to his chieftains. "The Drugars vastly outnumber us, and we have no way to replenish our arrows, once the supply we brought hither from Thandar has been exhausted."

"What do you suggest, my Omad?" asked Goran, one of the chieftains. "Should we break ranks and attack the Drugars in hand-to-hand combat?"

"That were suicidal," pointed out another of the chieftains, one Dumah. "For they are weightier than we, and mightier of limb. Still and all, it may be the only way to victory . . ."

Thus far in the battle, the warriors of Thandar had lost only a few lives, while inflicting heavy losses upon the Apemen of Kor. And Tharn was reluctant to waste his strength against the shambling horde.

"We shall see what happens," he growled. "After the next charge . . . and here they come!"

Hurok and I had fought beside the warriors of Thandar, and each of us had inflicted losses upon the enemy. I have no way of knowing what thoughts passed through the mind of my massive friend as he battled against his former compatriots, but I can imagine the emotions that stirred in his breast.

As for myself, I did not bother to waste the few bullets which remained to me, but employed a longbow I had taken from one of the slain Cro-Magnons. The weapon was cruder than those I had heretofore used in idle sport, but the skills I had learned in former days stood me well in the battle against the Neanderthals. More than one shaft loosed from my bow sank to the feather in the hairy breasts of a subhuman primitive.

When the next charge struck, it became instantly obvious to us all that Uruk was gambling his entire strength upon the chance of overwhelming our force. For he himself led the charge: too wary to expose himself to our bows, he had waited until our arrows were all but exhausted, before charging roaring in the vanguard, hoping to reap the victory.

And in truth we were almost out of arrows, and as for the spearsmen, their supply of javelins were very nearly depleted. And thus the defense disintegrated into a melee, as it became a hand-to-hand battle, with every man for himself.

And now the primitive Neanderthals had *us* at the disadvantage, for when it came to hand-to-hand battle, they were larger and stronger and very much heavier than we.

Amid the melee, I noticed a sudden trembling of the earth beneath our feet. I was swinging a stone axe in the very teeth of one of the Apemen, at the time. Splitting his ugly face in half and wrenching the stone blade of the axe free, I turned as the earth shook—

To see a fearsome sight!

I seized Tharn by the shoulder, as we fought side by side.

"Break and run for the trees!" I yelled in his ear. He stared uncomprehendingly, then followed the direction of my gaze and blanched.

Bellowing his command, he broke and ran for shelter, as did most of the well-disciplined Cro-Magnon warriors.

The Neanderthals, their blood-lust roused by now, paid

little attention, continuing to fight as long as a Thandarian stood before them to be slain. But when the line of defenders melted away in all directions, they turned bewilderedly.

"They flee!" howled Uruk, triumphantly. "We have won!"

As it happened, he stood directly in my path, the High Chief of the Apemen of Kor. And as I ran for shelter, he spied me and his little eyes gleamed. Leaping into my path, he attempted to brain me with one swing of his apelike arms.

I was, at the moment, unarmed, my spear having broken off short in the burly chest of the last Neanderthal I had slain and my arrows expended. But the automatic which Hurok had restored to me was still thrust within the waistband of my tattered shorts, and my hand went instinctively to the butt of the pistol as the immense form of Uruk loomed up before me, glee and blood-lust burning in his little eyes.

Then his gaze fell to the object in my fist, and his expression faltered. He recognized it from One-Eye's description as the terrible thunder-weapon. Sudden fear distorted his ugly visage, and he sought to hurl himself upon me before I could employ its magic against him.

I put a bullet through his brain.

The explosion seemed oddly loud—deafening! Arrested by the sudden noise, the Apemen paused, faltering. They wrinkled up their nostrils at the sharp, bitter, unfamiliar stench of gunpowder.

Uruk fell at my very feet as if struck down by some invisible force. Puzzled, his warriors looked him over, but their dim little eyes were not keen enough to discern the small, black-rimmed bullet-hole between his eyes. It must have seemed to the ghost-ridden and superstitious minds of the primitives that their mighty Chief had been felled by the force of magic!

Howling, they sprang away from me, clearing my path, and I seized the opportunity to sprint for the shelter of the trees while the hulking savages milled in confusion, their dull wits striving to ascertain what had felled their leader.

Now One-Eye leaped forward, snatched the fang necklace of the High Chief from about the thick, hairy throat of the carcass and clasped it about his own neck. The others blinked at him, dully.

"The panjani flee!" he yowled, spreading wide his heavy,

ape-like arms, brandishing his stone axe. "Fall upon them now, brave men of Kor, and slay them all!"

But still the earth shook and there sounded from the midst of the plain a drumming as of distant thunder coming near and nearer. One-Eye growled and cast a suspicious glance out into the flat land.

And at what he saw there, his face turned pale as milk beneath its coating of dirt and pelt of russet fur—!

Chapter 23.

THUNDERING DOOM!

Blinking with dazed relief in the sudden brilliance of day, Darya emerged from a cleft in the rock at the further side of the Peaks of Peril, gazing about her tremulously.

The cavern had indeed bisected the bulk of the mountain, and now the jungle girl stepped forth into the clean air and warm daylight, thankful to have escaped from the monsters of the mountain peaks.

She was weary and hungry and dirty and dishevelled, but she was also unharmed. Before her stretched a narrow strip of beach washed by the salty waves of the Sogar-Jad. A small stream of fresh water wound its way down the slope to mingle with the sea, and it was fringed on either side with dense bushes.

Glimpsing the gurgling little brook, the Cro-Magnon girl was suddenly mindful of her sorry condition. Dried blood from the carcass of the uld she had slain covered her back and shoulders, and her hands and arms and legs were filthy from crawling through black, noisome caves.

She paused and looked about her at the sloping ground, the narrow stretch of sandy beach, and the misty waters of the Sogar-Jad, which could be glimpsed shining through the interstices of the tall, fronded calamites which rose beside the prehistoric sea. Nowhere in view did the girl discern the slightest sign of animal or of human life, nor did aught her keen senses could detect suggest to her the presence of danger.

With a small sigh of relief, the weary girl unfastened her abbreviated garments of soiled, bedraggled fur, and cast them aside. For a moment she stood slim and naked at the edge of the little stream. Then she stepped daintily into the gurgling waters, waded out to the middle, and began to wash her beautiful young body.

The cold, pure water stung the many small cuts and abrasions on her arms, legs and knees, got from climbing through the stony caverns in the heart of the mountain. She splashed the chill water on her perfect breasts and scrubbed the dust and filth from her smooth thighs, sleek rounded calves and supple flanks, using handfulls of sand from the river-bottom in lieu of soap to scrub the stain of travel from her glowing flesh.

The icy wetness of her bath revived the flagging spirits of the Cro-Magnon princess and refreshed her weary and aching limbs. Floating on her back, she relaxed blissfully, enjoying her respite from exertion and danger.

That it might be only a momentary respite did not escape her thoughts; alas, it was to be even more brief than she could have guessed. . . .

As she relaxed, letting the cold waters of the gurgling stream lave and refresh her naked limbs, the young Cro-Magnon girl permitted her mind to drift back over the adventures and perils wherethrough she had so recently passed.

She wondered what had become of Jorn the Hunter and of the querulous, waspish old man from the Upper World . . . and her thoughts dwelt for a time on his tall, strong comrade with the crisp black hair and clear and steady gray eyes . . . did Eric Carstairs yet live, or had he succumbed to one or another of the numberless monsters of Zanthadon?

She rather hoped that somehow he had survived the many hazards of the wilderness . . . although it did not seem likely to her that she should ever set eyes upon him again.

Busied with her memories, letting the gushing river water drain the weariness and aching fatigue from her lithe young body, the girl dreamed lazily there, unmindful of the sharp, gloating eyes that lingered on her naked legs, sleek thighs and perfect young breasts.

From the concealment of the bushes which fringed the edges of the stream, a tall and curiously clad form crouched, staring at Darya through the leaves as she innocently bared her nude beauty amid the clear water.

The first sign she had that she was not alone came as swarthy hands clutched her bare shoulder and she turned to stare up into a cruel, grinning, bearded face.

And she *screamed*—

* * *

As One-Eye turned to seek the source of that perculiar
drumming thunder which caused the earth to shake, fear suddenly smote him to the heart and the power of speech
deserted his frozen tongue.

The stone axe he had clenched in his hairy hand now
dropped from his suddenly nerveless fingers as the Apeman
flinched in unholy terror from that which he saw bearing
down upon him upon the plain.

A long, moving mass of dark, lumbering forms, veiled in
rising dust, with the scarlet of crackling flames behind them,
goading them on!

Like moving mountains they were, like walking hills of
dark russet fur, their sail-like ears flapping, trunks lifted to
give voice to shrill squeals of sheer panic, and the daylight
gleamed dimly on their fantastic, curling tusks.

His tongue frozen with shock, all One-Eye could do to
warn his fellows was to extend one trembling arm and point
with numb and shaking fingers.

But from their secure niche behind the trees, Xask and Fumio saw his gesture. They had lurked here in safety, permitting the Drugars to charge the warriors of Thandar . . . and
now they were doubly glad they had not ventured forth from
the security of the jungle's edge.

By this time, all of the Cro-Magnon warriors had reached
the safety of the woods, and there were none left upon the
shallow little sandy knoll but the dead and some two score or
more of the victorious Drugars of Kor who had survived this
Stone Age version of Custer's Last Stand. Demoralized by the
inexplicable death of their High Chief, confused by the sudden flight of their enemies, the hulking Neanderthal men
milled about, and only a few saw what the speechless One-
Eye was pointing at.

They turned to stare . . . and froze with utter horror!

The enormous herd of giant wooly mammoths which Jorn
and the Professor had panicked into a stampede had traversed
the plain, and were coming down like thunder upon the
Apemen who stood, transfixed by fear, directly in the path of
the maddened brutes.

It is to be doubted if the lumbering pachyderms even noticed the Neanderthal men who occupied the place wherethrough they desired to pass. If the small eyes of the

mammoths did take notice, they cared little: for the fire was at their heels, its bitter, acrid smoke stinging their eyes and nostrils, and the fear of fire whelmed all other considerations from their maddened brains.

One-Eye uttered a shrill screech of terror, threw up his arms and vanished in a whirling cloud of dust as the first of the stampeding mammoths came thundering into the mob of confused, squalling Apemen.

Immense, padded feet drumming like thunder, shaking the earth, the stampede passed through and over the crowd of warriors, trampling them into the gore-drenched dust.

Only the barrier of the trees turned the stampede aside. For the great boles were set too thickly together for even the lumbering juggernauts to crush them down.

Within minutes, the herd had passed, leaving gory ruin behind where had stood the victorious Drugars of Kor. The mammoths dwindled in the distance, slowing their frenzied pace as the smoke left their nostrils. Slowing to a shuffle, the huge bulls ambled out into the plains again, guarding the females and the young.

A sudden drizzle soaked through the trees—one of those frequent, brief cloudbursts which arise so swiftly in the humid air and cloudy skies of Zanthodon.

The warm rain sluiced the earth, saturating the trampled grasses. The coals of the racing grassfire died to hissing embers.

The fire was over; and so was the invasion from Kor.

Lurking in the trees, Xask and Fumio exchanged a long glance.

"Let us begone from this place," suggested the former vizier of Kor.

"A good idea," agreed Fumio. "But where shall we go?"

"Anywhere else but here," whispered Xask with an eloquent glance at the middle distance, where the warriors of Thandar were emerging from the underbrush to search for survivors and for unbroken weapons wherewith to arm themselves.

A while later, having retrieved those of the arrows and spears which had remained unbroken when the trampling feet of the herd had driven them deep into the soft, spongy soil of the knoll, the warriors of Thandar entered the jungle again and sought a suitable place to make their camp and consider what next they should do.

When the last of the Cro-Magnons had vanished into the jungle, loose dirt heaved, and a filthy shape lurched into view, gasping for air but thankful to be alive.

It was none other than One-Eye! Somehow, miraculously, the Drugar chieftain had evaded the crushing feet of the trampling pachyderms by wedging his hairy body into a small gully. Later, when the hated Cro-Magnons had come to retrieve those of their weapons which had survived unbroken, the fearful Apeman had feigned death. Among so many broken, crushed corpses, the Thandarians may perchance be forgiven for overlooking one which yet lived.

Peering fearfully about, One-Eye scampered into the jungle, and clambered up a broad-limbed tree to rest and recover his courage. That he was the last of his kind on the mainland he knew all too well, for surely all of his fellows had been crushed to death under the feet of the stampeding mammoths.

From his perch atop a broad and level branch, he watched with red murder flaming in his one eye as the hated panjani strode down the jungle paths, disappearing amid the trees.

Among them he spied Eric Carstairs and Hurok the traitor.

And in his cruel and evil heart, the Neanderthal man swore to be avenged upon his enemies.

Chapter 24.

SCARLET SAILS

Suddenly, Jorn the Hunter froze, straining every nerve and listening intently.

"Hark!" wheezed Professor Potter at his side. "What was *that?*"

"I do not know," Jorn muttered shortly. "It sounded like a woman screaming in mortal fear—"

The two had traced the narrow and winding gorge through the Peaks of Peril, until they had almost reached the farther side of the cliffs. They had been maneuvering their way through the stone walls of the little pass, when suddenly there had come to their ears the faint cry from the distance.

"Could it be the young woman?" murmured the Professor fearfully.

The glint of fear came and went in the steady blue eyes of the Cro-Magnon warrior at his side.

"I do not know," he grunted. "But it was a woman's voice, and what woman could possibly exist in this desolate region, swarming with monstrous thakdols, if not the gomad Darya?"

Straining his ears to catch the slightest sound, the stalwart youth stood motionless for another long moment. Then, turning to his companion, he said:

"Come!"

And with that curt word, the Stone Age youth broke into a rapid, space-eating stride, racing in the general direction from which there had come to his ears that sharp, frightened cry of a woman's fear.

They had evidently penetrated farther down the narrow pass between the Peaks of Peril than even Jorn the Hunter had guessed, for it was only a few minutes later that the close-set walls gave way and the warrior and the old scientist found themselves in the open country again.

Before them stretched a prospect of sandy slope leading

down to the shore of the Sogar-Jad. A stand of tall calamites blocked most of their view of the inland sea, and the only other thing to meet their eyes was a small gurgling brook which meandered between shores lined with thick shrubbery, emptying into the sea.

Searching about with eagle eyes, Jorn suddenly became aware of that which rode the mist-veiled waves of the prehistoric ocean.

And his keen eyes widened incredulously, as he stared upon a sight so fantastic as to beggar comparison—

For the better part of two hours, Kâiradine Redbeard, called Barbarossa, and seventh in direct succession from the famous Khair ud-Din of Algiers, had watched as his longboats fetched to their ship supplies of fresh game, fruit and water.

The tall, long-legged reis or captain of the pirate galley at length decided to stretch his legs upon the shore himself, and set out with the last boatload of his corsairs. Beaching the boat upon the sandy strand, he strode inland, glad to feel the firm land beneath his feet once more, after two months at sea.

Anchored off the shoals, his galley, the *Red Witch*, swayed to the rhythm of the waves. He surveyed his pirate galley, approvingly, the red sails booming and snapping in the breeze, the green banner of Islam fluttering from the stern. For many weeks had the Barbary pirate been at sea; soon, now, he would head his prow farther up along the coast, returning in triumph to his home port.

By now the last kegs of fresh water and barrels of ripe fruit had been borne into the longboat, and it was nearly time to depart; for the Moslem pirate did not care to linger for too long a time in the vicinity of the Peaks of Peril, mindful of the dreaded thakdols that made their nests amid that wilderness of cleft and soaring rock.

He was a commanding figure as he stood there, looking about him. His curled beard was tinted red with dyes, and stank of heavy perfumes; his lean, muscular body was swathed in the long robes of the desert princes who had been his remote forebears. His swarthy, hook-nosed face was villainous, but not unhandsome in a fierce, hawklike, imperious way. From the curled toes of his red-leather boots to his linen headdress, he was every inch a swaggering figure stepped forth from the golden pages of romance.

A rustling in the bushes came to his alert senses. Laying

the long fingers of one swarthy, beringed hand upon the hilt of his scimitar, he glanced through the leaves . . . and at what he saw, his eyes widened delightedly.

"By the Veiled Prophet of Khorassan—*a girl!*" he swore softly. And his eyes glided over the slim naked body, the sleek thighs and firm, luscious breasts of the blond-haired girl who splashed carelessly in the waters of the little stream.

Passion flared within the breast of the Barbary pirate as he stood there, concealed by the bushes, watching as Darya of Thandar bathed.

Passion, and . . . *desire!*

And, with such swaggering, lawless rogues as Kâiradine of El-Cazar, to desire was to—*possess.*

Darya was unconscious of the presence of another as she splashed nakedly in the little stream until suddenly the bushes parted to reveal the tall, curiously-garbed figure of a grinning man.

He plunged into the stream and bore down upon her, and the Cro-Magnon girl had time to scream only once before strong fingers closed about her mouth and sinewy arms crushed her in a powerful embrace. . . .

Having been alarmed by that terrified shriek, Jorn the Hunter and Professor Potter had traversed the remainder of the pass at a rapid pace, and now stood transfixed with astonishment at the unexpected sight which met their eyes.

The Stone Age savage uttered a stifled gasp at the enormous thing before him; a moment later, his keen gaze narrowed and a growl of primeval menace sounded from his deep breast.

As for the elderly savant, he was too amazed to utter a sound.

Before them lay a prospect of sea and shore, with tall trees beyond, and a small river. But it was none of these commonplace and natural features of the landscape which caught and seized their fascinated attention.

There, riding at anchor off-shore, rose a red-sailed galley such as neither of the two men had ever seen before in all their lives. At the sight of this amazing ship, the Stone Age boy blinked as if stunned.

And the Professor gaped incredulously. For, if he had never seen such a craft in the flesh, so to speak, he had seen its likeness depicted many times before, in books and paintings.

"By my soul," he stammered feebly, "a pirate ship—a galley! (See the oarbanks?)—and Islamic, from the green banner at the stern . . . Artful Archimedes: *the Barbaray pirates!*"

And there came crowding into the Professor's dazed and wondering brain the history of those daring and villainous sea rovers, who had roamed and ruled the coastal waters of North Africa from Algiers to Tunis, led by the dreaded redbeard, Barbarossa, until driven from their island strongholds by the French conquest of Algeria in 1830.

But—Barbary pirates here in Zanthodon?

"Well, and after all, why not?" murmured the Professor vaguely. They could, after all, have fled inland to avoid the French fleets, finding their way overland to the Ahaggar Mountains, and to the hollow crater of the extinct volcano . . . as obviously they or their ancestors had, nearly a century and a half ago.

"See! It is the gomad Darya," cried Jorn, pointing suddenly. The Professor peered, his heart sinking: tall, swarthy sailors were lifting aboard from a longboat the naked and struggling body of a young white woman with long bright hair the color of sun-ripened corn and wide blue eyes like the skies of April. It could be none other than Darya—

Without a word, Jorn burst into a run. Across the slope he hurtled, and down the shore, to fling his strong bronzed body into the tossing waves of the Sogar-Jad.

As the half-naked, brawny body of the Cro-Magnon warrior clove the waves of the Sogar-Jad, heading directly toward the sides of the great pirate galley, the sailors along the rail caught sight of their unexpected visitor and called the attention of their captain, who had just come aboard with his naked, and furiously struggling, captive.

"O reis Kâiradine! Behold!" they shouted, pointing.

The hawklike gaze of the Barbaray pirate narrowed; he could not help admiring the reckless courage of the savage boy to strive single-handedly to rescue his jungle sweetheart. But his numbers were already depleted by battle with the Apemen of Kor and other savage peoples he had encounterd during his voyage.

He raised his jewelled hand carelessly, and at the signal his pirates quickly unlimbered their horn bows, nocking barbed and deadly arrows and drawing the feathered shafts tight.

Oblivious to his danger, the young warrior of Thandar

swam to the side of the pirate craft, and had just reached it when the misty waves of the sea were ripped and torn by a deadly rain of hissing arrows.

The waves burst into seething froth as Jorn kicked and struggled. Then his body sank beneath the waters of the prehistoric sea, and vanished from sight.

"Cast off, my corsairs!" cried Kâiradine Redbeard. And as the anchor rose dripping from the Sogar-Jad and strong hands tugged the sails into position, and the sharp keel of the galley swung about for El-Cazar, the Barbary pirate seized up his helpless captive and bore within his cabin the naked form of Darya of Thandar.

The cabin door thudded shut behind them, muffling her sudden scream of terror.

And on the shores of the Sogar-Jad, an old man in dilapidated and travel-stained garments fell forward weakly to his knees and buried his face in shaking hands.

Darya carried off by pirates, and Jorn slain! And, he, himself, alone and friendless in a savage world of prehistoric monsters and primitive fighting men!

It was too much even for the brave and gallant spirit of Professor Percival P. Potter. And the old scientist fell forward in a dead faint, there at the feet of the Peaks of Peril, by the shores of the prehistoric sea.

THE END

But the Adventures of
Eric Carstairs in
the Underground World will continue in
"ZANTHODON,"
the second volume in this new series.

Appendix

A STONE AGE GLOSSARY

DRUGAR: Literally, "Ugly One." The Cro-Magnons' name for the Neanderthals.

DRUNTH. The stegosaurus.

GOMAD. The title of the daughter of a High Chief, or Omad. Has much the same meaning as "princess."

GOROTH. The mighty bull aurochs of the Ice Ages, resembling the bison.

GRYMP. Triceratops, one of the more terrible of the Jurassic dinosaurs.

JAD. The word for "sea"; also, "water."

JAMAD. The son of an Omad, or High Chief; literally, "prince."

LUGAR. A word meaning "smaller" or "lesser," as in Lugar-Jad, the Lesser Sea.

OMAD. The High Chief or ruler of a country; literally, "king."

OMODON. The giant cave bear of Ice Age Europe, larger and fiercer than the grizzly.

PANJAN. Literally "Smoothskin." The Neanderthals' name for the Cro-Magnons. The plural is *panjani.*

SOGAR. A superlative: "great" or "greater," as in Sogar-Jad, the Greater Sea.

SUJAT. Anything which the peoples of Zanthodon regard with superstitious awe is considered *sujat.* The word has much the same meaning as both "sacred" and "supernatural."

THAKDOL. A pterodactyl, the great flying lizard of the Jurassic Age.

THANTOR. The wooly mammoth of Ice Age Europe.

ULD. A small, plump, harmless mammal. Eric Carstairs is of the opinion that the uld may be eohippus, the remote ancestor of the horses of today. The people of Thandar and, perhaps, of Kor, may hunt or even breed the uld for meat.

VANDAR. The great saber-tooth tiger of the Stone Age, one of the most feared and cunning of all the predators of the jungles of Zanthodon.

VATOR. The word for "father" in the universal language of Zanthodon. The word for "mother" is not given in the text, but may be *mator*.

VATHRIB. A species of gigantic albino spider which inhabits the subterranean depths.

XUNTH. Enormous serpents, dwelling in caverns in the mountains.

YITH. The dragon-snake of the primordial seas of Zanthodon, which Professor Potter has identified with the extinct plesiosaurus.

ZOMAK. A primitive species of feathered bird-reptile, which Eric Carstairs considers to be the archaeopteryx.

DAW BOOKS presents . . .

LIN CARTER

The Green Star series

☐	UNDER THE GREEN STAR	(#UW1433—$1.50)
☐	WHEN THE GREEN STAR CALLS	(#UY1267—$1.25)
☐	BY THE LIGHT OF THE GREEN STAR	(#UY1268—$1.25)
☐	AS THE GREEN STAR RISES	(#UY1156—$1.25)
☐	IN THE GREEN STAR'S GLOW	(#UY1399—$1.25)

The Gondwane series

☐	THE WARRIOR OF WORLD'S END	(#UW1420—$1.50)
☐	THE ENCHANTRESS OF WORLD'S END	(#UY1172—$1.25)
☐	THE IMMORTAL OF WORLD'S END	(#UY1254—$1.25)
☐	THE BARBARIAN OF WORLD'S END	(#UW1300—$1.50)
☐	THE PIRATE OF WORLD'S END	(#UW1410—$1.75)

plus

☐	THE WIZARD OF ZAO	(#UE1383—$1.75)

DAW BOOKS are represented by the publishers of Signet and Mentor Books, **THE NEW AMERICAN LIBRARY, INC.**

THE NEW AMERICAN LIBRARY, INC.,
P.O. Box 999, Bergenfield, New Jersey 07621

Please send me the DAW BOOKS I have checked above. I am enclosing
$_____ (check or money order—no currency or C.O.D.'s).
Please include the list price plus 50¢ per order to cover handling costs.

Name _____

Address _____

City _____ State _____ Zip Code _____
Please allow at least 4 weeks for delivery